THE UN̲LISTED

BOOK TWO – REBELLION

THE *UNLISTED*

BOOK TWO – REBELLION

JUSTINE FLYNN   CHRIS KUNZ

■SCHOLASTIC

Published in the UK by Scholastic Children's Books, 20XX
Euston House, 24 Eversholt Street, London, NW1 1DB, UK
A division of Scholastic Limited.

London – New York – Toronto – Sydney – Auckland
Mexico City – New Delhi – Hong Kong

SCHOLASTIC and associated logos are trademarks and/or
registered trademarks of Scholastic Inc.

ISBN 978 0702 30161 2

A CIP catalogue record for this book is available from the British Library.

Printed by CPI Group (UK) Ltd, Croydon, CR0 4YY
Papers used by Scholastic Children's Books are made
from wood grown in sustainable forests.

1 3 5 7 9 10 8 6 4 2

www.scholastic.co.uk

Dedicated to the young people who are brave enough to question the status quo — the future belongs to you

CHAPTER ONE

At Circular Quay, tourists mingled with office workers as everyone hurriedly went about their day in the beautiful summer sunshine. The roof of the Sydney Opera House gleamed white against the blue of the harbour as passengers disembarked by the hundreds, listening to the muffled instructions over the loudspeaker for the times of departing and arriving ferries. Electronic plastic cards had to be scanned before commuters were allowed on and off the ferries. From all corners and angles surveillance cameras monitored the flow of people and acted as a deterrent to pickpockets.

In a busy city such as this, it was hard to go anywhere without being monitored.

Even though it was early, the buskers on the Quay were already in place. One of the regulars, a silver-painted statue, stood absolutely still on his pedestal. Tourists stopped and stared at him, willing him to move. Only when they threw money in the basket at his feet did he wave or bow in thanks.

As the crowds waxed and waned, no-one took any notice of the teenage girl closely watching the performance and scanning the crowd. Kymara, a thirteen-year-old Indigenous girl and one of the Unlisted, wore a hoodie that obscured her face. She clocked that the busker had a bag resting on the ground near a bench. His mobile phone was just there, in plain sight.

She strolled over to the bench and casually sat down, pretending to bend to tie her shoelace. Heart pounding, she grabbed the busker's phone and stood up and strolled away in the direction of the nearby glass lift that took pedestrians from Quay level up to the Cahill Expressway.

While Kymara waited impatiently for the lift to come, she wasted no time, bringing up the passcode override screen and typing in a few digits. Moments later, she had bypassed the phone's password lock and accessed her online account. She was supposed to be collecting food for breakfast, not borrowing and hacking phones, but before she could talk herself out of her plan, the lift door opened and she stepped inside. So far, so good.

Life had changed so much for her in the past week; nothing she did now felt like the kind of thing a normal Australian teenager would have ever even contemplated.

It had all started with a nationwide rollout of a dental check, which Kymara had avoided because she hated dentists. No biggie, right? Wrong. It turned out that the dentist check involved implanting a child with a device. And when they'd worked out that Kymara hadn't been implanted, a day later she'd been rounded up like some kind of common criminal by security guards who were employed by an organisation called the Infinity Group. On the way to who knows where, the van she and the other three kids – all total strangers – were travelling in, crashed. Without a word spoken, she and the other teens made a run for it.

And they'd been hiding out in the city ever since, in the underground tunnel system underneath St James train station.

Before all this, Kymara's whole life had been online. She was a gamer, and her YouTube videos were watched by thousands of kids all over the world. It was who she was and what she liked most in the world. Sure, she did boring things like go to school and clean her room, but she lived for technology, gaming and her fans. And now she'd been banned from talking or posting or gaming or doing everything that required an internet connection. Because the Infinity Group seemed to have eyes and ears everywhere and for reasons they were still finding out, they wanted every kid in Australia implanted with a device.

The four runaways made friends via a dodgy

walkie-talkie frequency with two identical twins, Dru and Kal Sharma, who were helping them find out more about what was going on. One of the twins, Dru, hated the dentist as much as Kymara did, and had avoided the dental check. In fact, he'd got his brother to pretend to be him, not having any idea how that would change both their lives.

So now Kal was being affected by two implants, and Infinity Group hadn't worked out yet that Dru had not been implanted at all. Which meant as long as they were careful, Dru could remain above ground and close to Kal.

It was all so crazy and far-fetched that if Kymara thought about it too much, her head might explode. This was Australia after all. A nice, safe, sunny, democratic place to live with plenty of food and jobs for everyone. And yet, something sinister and terrifying was happening to kids right under the noses of everyone, and adults were oblivious to it.

Kymara couldn't just live underground in a dirty tunnel wearing second-hand clothes scrounged from a charity bin and hope for the best. It wasn't in her nature to give up. Which was why she was above ground and doing something Rose, Jacob and Gemma might not be thrilled about. But she'd spent all night thinking it through and she knew the plan was a good one.

Once the lift door closed, the noise of Circular Quay dimmed and it gave her the quiet she needed. Taking a big steadying breath, Kymara pulled her hood down, held the phone out, pressed record, and slipped instantly into her online gaming persona.

'Greetings gamers, coders and decoders. Today we're going retro. Your girl Kymara coming at you live from this beautiful lift that smells like wee. Sorry about the hiatus – school's been a real kick in the teeth lately. I can't be alone on that, right?' Kymara held a finger to her lips, revealing the letters *SSP?* written along the side of her finger.

'I want your *letters* to the editor, so hit me up in the comments and let me know I'm not the only *Steve* in *Zomville*. Peace and love!' She made a peace sign, once again revealing the scrawled *SSP?* on her finger, and ended the video as the lift returned to ground level.

Kymara pulled up her hood and darted back out to the quay. She passed behind the busker and surreptitiously dropped the phone onto the top of his bag. The busker remained motionless – which wasn't surprising, really – as Kymara ran to a cement pylon and hid behind it.

Glancing back in the direction of the busker, she saw two Infinity Group guards dressed in black, zero in on the busker. Not moving was no longer an option for the poor guy as the guards literally carried him and his bag away, with him shouting and kicking.

Nearby tourists seemed to think this was just an interesting twist in the busker's performance, but Kymara knew better. She felt terrible for what had happened. It was her fault but she didn't think they would hold him for very long. After all, he'd done nothing but stand still.

Kymara waited until the busker and guards had disappeared from sight, then, head down, she returned home to the tunnels.

CHAPTER TWO

The classroom at Westbrook High School was bubbling with chatter as kids discussed homework and last night's footy scores. Kal and Dru Sharma were quietly observing their friend Tim. He was sitting alone, not engaged with the action happening around him.

'You should go check on him,' said Dru to his twin. 'See if he's heard from his parents.'

Kal looked sullen. He never liked his brother telling him what to do. 'I've tried. He's not talking to me.'

Dru and Kal were still coming to terms with everything that had happened over the last few days but so much didn't make sense. After finding out that their aunt was now working for the Global Child Initiative, they knew they'd have to be more careful than ever.

All of a sudden, the room stilled. Dru stiffened, looking at his brother and classmates out of the corner of his eye. Kal's eyes were glazed over and his fingers were twitching, just like every other student in the class. It was happening again!

Dru immediately mimicked his brother's actions, while also looking around cautiously to check the other students. They were all frozen, except –

A new boy had entered the classroom and was staring at the students. He looked about the same age as Dru and Kal. He was tall, Asian and wore a smart black blazer. Dru had never laid eyes on him before.

Moments later Miss Biggs entered the room. The school's Wellness Officer glanced at the class, looking pleased. Checking her tablet, she tapped away briefly, finishing just as the students returned to normal. Miss Biggs stood next to the new boy at the front of the class, holding her tablet and looking around the room expectantly.

Then, in unison, all the students except for Dru started to speak in Mandarin. Dru tried not to let his shock show. It was a language the class had been studying since the start of the year but most of the students hadn't got past struggling with basic pronunication. But now, they all chanted: *'Yuyán gengxin wánchéng.'*

Dru quickly joined in, 'Uh . . . *wánchéng.'* Dru again noticed the new boy watching him suspiciously. But Miss Biggs smiled, clearly pleased with the class's sudden newfound language skills.

'Hello, class –' Miss Biggs stopped as she noticed Regan Holcroft's gaze still fixed straight ahead, statue-like, her fingers twitching.

The Wellness Officer frowned as Regan started to slump in her chair and slide off. But before she hit the floor the new boy leapt over to steady her. Regan regained full consciousness, and seemed utterly embarrassed to find someone she had never seen before making a fuss of her.

Miss Biggs looked to the new boy. 'Thank you for your help, Jiao.' She eyed Regan closely. 'Regan, could you please visit the sick bay after class?'

Regan looked mortified at being seen to show weakness. She shook her head. 'I'm fine, Miss, really, just a little tired.'

Miss Biggs stared at her before stating firmly, 'I'm sure you're fine, Regan. We'll just double-check.'

Regan grimaced – it was clear Miss Biggs was not going to take no for an answer – but said nothing else.

Miss Biggs returned her focus to the rest of the class. 'I was about to say, please join me in welcoming Jiao Yang. He's here from China as part of the Global Child Initiative's Leadership Exchange Program. Jiao's a Year Leader back in China, like Regan. So, he will also be one while he's here in Australia.'

Dru and Kal shared a quick look, thinking the same thought. China was participating in the Global Child Initiative too?

Regan scowled at the overseas exchange student, which caused Dru to grin. He knew Regan disliked any sort of competition, and this Jiao kid had only been in the class a few minutes and he'd already made her look bad in front of Miss Biggs.

The Global Child Initiative's Wellness Officer looked at her watch with a frown, and continued. 'Your class teacher is obviously running late. Jiao, why don't you give a quick maths quiz in Mandarin?'

Jiao smiled and nodded.

Dru watched the outrage open on Regan's face. Clearly she was not going to take this lying down. She stood up, confidently. 'Or should I do it, Miss Biggs? Considering *I'm* the actual Year Leader?'

She looked over at Jiao smugly until Miss Biggs responded with, 'That won't be necessary, Regan.'

Regan sat down, tossing Kal a foul look as he sniggered.

Miss Biggs nodded. 'Take it away, Jiao.'

Kal looked over at his brother, amused. 'This shouldn't take long. We suck at Mandarin.'

Dru, trying to bury the unease caused by what he'd seen this morning, raised an eyebrow. 'Ha, speak for yourself.' Dru had always excelled at languages, and he was one of the best in the class at Mandarin.

Jiao started calling out questions in Mandarin. 'Is sixty-one a prime or composite number?'

Dru was about to answer when Tim Hale piped up with the correct answer, in Mandarin.

Dru slowly turned to Tim, who looked blankly ahead of him. Tim had never been a bright student. He'd always been more into sports. Just last week he'd failed a very easy spot quiz in Mandarin. So, what was going on now?

Jiao looked pleased, and then asked the class another question. 'What is the highest common factor of eighteen and six?'

Dru was equally confused when Chloe answered perfectly in Mandarin.

Jiao turned to Kal and asked, 'What is the square root of zero?'

Dru watched on in amazement as his brother answered without hesitation. Even Kal looked surprised by his own polished response.

Jiao saw Dru's incredulous expression, and asked him a question in Mandarin. 'What is sixty-four divided by sixteen?'

Dru panicked, unsure of the answer. Instead, he blurted out the first phrase that popped into his head. *'Fei cháng gan xiè ni!'*

Straightaway the class fell about laughing, and Jiao joined in, while Miss Biggs observed the class silently. He moved closer to Dru's desk and said in English, 'I asked you to divide sixty-four by sixteen, and you said . . . "thank you very much".'

Dru wanted to sink into the floor. This was the most embarrassing thing that had ever happened to him in the classroom. He had always been the smart one, the one with the right answer in class. This was the stuff his nightmares were made from.

Seeing his brother's distress, Kal spoke in Mandarin to Jiao. 'He's a very polite boy, sir.'

Jiao looked at both twins and then chose to accept Kal's excuse and resumed his maths quiz in Mandarin.

Kal leant over to his brother and whispered, 'I totally covered for you, bro. You owe me.'

Dru was perplexed. 'I don't get it. I'm the only one in class who's any good at Mandarin.'

But as Xavier answered another of Jiao's maths questions correctly in Mandarin, he had to rethink. '. . . or I was,' he said to his brother.

Mr Park entered the room to find the class already started and Miss Biggs taking notes. Miss Biggs gave him a cold smile. 'Nice of you to join us, Mr Park. The class is all yours.' She strode out of the room and Jiao walked down the back of the class and took the empty seat next to Tim Hale.

Dru was relieved to see the back of Miss Biggs. He turned to his brother. 'Kal, we have to get back on the network to find out what they've got planned. I can't keep playing catch-up, or next time I'll really get busted.'

CHAPTER **THREE**

CHAPTER **THREE**

Dru and Kal snuck along the pathway, trying to appear invisible or, at the very least, innocent. It was morning recess, and they only had a few minutes. As usual, Dru had come up with a plan and hadn't bothered to tell his brother what it was.

Up ahead the school cleaner pushed his cleaning trolley, humming happily as he went about his business. The cleaner slowed down, and the boys quickly moved against the side wall, hoping the cleaner hadn't seen them.

The cleaner unlocked the staffroom door, grabbed

a few cleaning supplies and headed inside. Dru looked pleased and nodded towards the trolley. Kal stared back at Dru with a raised eyebrow. 'Can you tell me what we're doing sneaking around – and what we want with the cleaner?' he asked, annoyed at being kept in the dark yet again.

Dru glared at his brother and held his finger to his lips using the international sign for *shush*. 'It's a need-to-know scenario, and right now you don't need to know.'

Dru edged forward a step so he could see into the staffroom. He saw a Roomba-like vacuum zipping across the carpet, and punched the air with delight. 'Perfect!'

Dru watched as the cleaner bent down, picked it up and headed towards the exit. He jumped back behind the wall, out of sight. 'He's got it with him,' Dru whispered, delighted.

Kal just rolled his eyes, still completely unaware of what his brother was going on about.

The cleaner was now walking down the corridor,

pushing his cleaning trolley, and Dru signalled to Kal that they should follow.

The boys watched as the cleaner wheeled the trolley into a supply room before locking the door with a padlock and walking away.

Once the cleaner was out of sight, Dru and Kal moved over to the locked door. Dru groaned when he saw the padlock. 'Great. How are we going to get in now?'

Kal reached out and easily snapped the padlock off the door. 'Like this,' he said with a smug smile.

Dru didn't offer Kal the congratulations Kal knew he deserved, and instead just opened the door to the supply room, carefully closing it behind them. Dru found the vacuum cleaner, and picked it up while Kal looked on.

'Dude, what are you doing? Have you suddenly developed a passion for cleaning? Dadi will be impressed.'

Dru tried not to smile, and decided to put his brother out of his misery. 'This thing,' he said, lifting up the vacuum cleaner, 'is our chance to hack into the school system.'

Kal frowned. 'You're going to hack into a floor cleaner?'

'Yeah, but it's not just any old floor cleaner. It's a smart device, and no-one will know we've accessed the school system through this because it's not alarmed.'

'Smart move, bro,' responded Kal, impressed. 'Although you better not get caught out like you did last time.'

Dru rolled his eyes while pulling his laptop out of his backpack, placing it carefully on a stack of toilet paper beside the door. Kal loved to bring up the time his twin had hacked into the school records to boost a couple of Chloe's text scores. He'd got found out and had received an official caution from the school and a technology ban from his parents.

Dru was busy typing away but it was taking longer than Kal was comfortable with. 'You know we have year assembly in two minutes, right?' he reminded Dru.

His twin didn't answer. Dru brought up a screen

and quickly read it, equally horrified and delighted with what he'd discovered. He looked at his brother. 'Remember this morning when you all came out of zombie mode, you said *"Yuyán gēngxīn wánchéng".*'

Kal nodded. 'Yes. "Language update complete".'

'Right. And see here?' he pointed to the screen, which read: *Language update. 9.23 a.m.* He flicked over to another screen. 'And they have updates planned for every day this week!'

'Right . . . well, that's kind of interesting, but right now I'm more worried about what will happen if we miss assembly. We have to go.'

'Not yet,' replied Dru. 'I want to see if I can find out what happened to you when you almost fainted in the tunnels yesterday. This might be our only chance.'

'I didn't faint,' said Kal, never wanting to admit to any weakness.

Dru brought up a screen of diagnostics, with Kal's photo, full of information on his whereabouts. But there was an obvious break in the data, which coincided with the time Kal was underground. 'Look at this. You dropped out of the system. No tracking, no enhanced strength. That must be why you collapsed.' Dru was enjoying learning more information about the implant. 'So . . . the tunnels are really the best place for Rose and the others to be.'

'Come *on*,' said Kal, tapping his watch.

Dru held up a hand. 'Wait a moment. I want to check on Bua, find out what Infinity Group is planning.'

But at that moment the door to the supply room creaked open. Dru grabbed his laptop, and both boys ducked behind the towering stack of toilet paper.

Kal carefully peered out to see the new exchange student, Jiao, standing with his back to the twins, rummaging around, clearly searching for something. Kal didn't waste a moment. He darted out and lifted Jiao and upended him into an industrial laundry trolley filled with school washing. Jiao was upside-down before he could even speak. 'Hey, what –'

Under normal circumstances, the boys would have taken a moment to laugh about this – but this was not the time to stop for a chuckle.

Dru disconnected his laptop cable from the vacuum cleaner and the twins raced out of the room.

•

Kal and Dru ran into the quadrangle to find their year group already in line, led of course by Regan, who had taken her customary position at the head.

'That was too close!' Kal hissed to Dru as they jumped in between students.

Dru agreed. 'Sorry. And thanks for your quick thinking. But why was that kid looking in the supply room? Was he following us?'

Kal shrugged. 'Do you think he was just interested in the school's toilet-paper supply?' he asked sarcastically. Then he looked pointedly in the direction of where the boys had just come from. Dru turned to see Jiao run into the quadrangle, looking flustered. He took his place next to Regan at the head of the line.

The twins weren't the only ones to notice Jiao's dishevelled arrival.

22

'Sir,' said Regan, raising her hand to get Mr Park's attention. 'Jiao was late to assembly.'

Mr Park gave Regan a resigned look. 'Thank you, Regan. Let me worry about who's late.'

Regan shot a dirty look in Jiao's direction, but Jiao just stared back, impassive.

CHAPTER FOUR

Inside the tunnels, Rose tied her long dark hair back with an old rubber band. Around her neck was the golden locket she had worn since her parents gave it to her on her twelfth birthday. She hadn't bothered changing out of the same red checked flannelette shirt and khaki trousers she'd been wearing for a few days now. What was the point? Everything became dirty down in the tunnels. Jacob and Gemma were piling the day's food haul into the middle of their new hide-out.

A hungry Jacob was particularly excited with the pile of food. 'Noodles, egg, peanuts. I could make such an awesome pad thai with this, if we had electricity.' He rubbed his hands on his faded camouflage shorts.

Kymara walked in wearing a cotton button-down shirt and ripped black jeans, looking relaxed and upbeat but empty-handed. 'What up, my peeps?' she asked the others.

'Where have you been?' asked Rose, annoyed. 'We were starting to get worried.'

Gemma added. 'We all got back ages ago. What were you doing?' She noticed another smudge on her glasses, took them off and polished them on the sleeve of her old floral blouse.

'And where's your food?' Jacob finished.

Kymara shrugged. 'These are all great questions, and they have great answers. But first, I'm starving.' She moved to grab a bruised apple from the pile but Rose held up her hand.

'Okay, okay,' said Kymara, reading the angry expressions on their faces and deciding she needed to get this out of the way sooner rather than later. 'I know you're going to freak, but this is actually amazing news: I posted a new video.'

'You *what*?' said Rose, wide-eyed as the other two just looked at Kymara in horror.

'Chill, guys. I knew you'd react like this. I did it from a stranger's phone, so it's not linked to us. Infinity Group must be monitoring the account though, because they stormed straight in and searched the dude I'd taken the phone from. I feel bad about that.'

'And this is why we didn't want you to go out on your own.' Rose spoke first, trying to control her temper. 'We can't trust you.'

Gemma was near tears. 'You put us all at risk for the sake of a few likes?'

Kymara was indignant. 'A hundred thousand hits per video is not a few likes, Gemma,' she retorted, before quickly moving on. 'But I didn't do it for that reason, okay.'

The others just stared at her.

'The piece I recorded had a secret code in it, to signal to other kids who might be in the same situation as us.'

She waited a moment so the others could see the genius in her plan.

No-one spoke.

'Pretty clever, huh?' she prompted them.

For a minute, it looked as though the group was coming around, but then Jacob asked a question.

'Where's the walkie-talkie? You took it with you, right?'

The colour drained from Kymara's face as she realised her big mistake and the jeopardy she had put them all in. 'The walkie-talkie? I, ah, put my backpack down when I went to take the phone. And I . . .' She didn't want to finish the sentence but knew she must. 'I . . . might have left it on the bench next to the busker at Circular Quay.'

Rose no longer bothered to hide her anger. 'Just to be clear,' she seethed, 'you left a walkie-talkie linked to Kal and Dru – with your fingerprints on it – in a place swarming with Infinity Group agents?'

Kymara didn't know what to say. 'Um, yep. God, I feel terrible.'

Rose looked to the others, determined. 'We're going back to retrieve that walkie-talkie before Infinity Group does.' She looked at the others. 'And we need to go now.'

'In my defence,' Kymara began, 'can I just say –'

But before she could finish the sentence the other three responded with a short, sharp collective, 'No!'

•

At the end of the day Dru and Kal walked their bikes out of school. At the gate Jiao stood alone, watching the twins. 'See you soon, Dru,' he said pointedly, ignoring Kal.

Dru tried not to panic and, not trusting himself to speak without sounding fearful, he looked down and continued walking. As soon as they were out of earshot Dru turned to his brother. '*See you soon*? What does that mean? Why is he picking on *me*?'

Kal scoffed. 'Dru, you're overreacting. Maybe he was just trying to make friends.'

Dru was about to disagree vehemently when the

twins' neighbour, Chloe, approached them, phone in hand. As usual, her red hair was pulled back in plaits and her expression was animated. 'Check it out, Dru,' she said, showing Dru her screen. 'Kymara posted another video! Kind of a strange one too.'

The twins shared a quick, surreptitious look of concern, both eager to hide their feelings from Chloe. Before Dru could reply, Regan suddenly appeared behind them. 'Chloe, I need to talk to you,' she said primly, then glanced at the boys and sneered. 'Hey, Sharmas. Still spending every minute together?'

'So what?' Dru snapped back, trying to calm his growing nerves. 'We're twins.'

Kal just shook his head at his brother and then said quietly so only he could hear. 'Come on, we've got to get home and check out that video.' Without another word, Kal jumped on his bike and cycled away.

Dru gave Chloe a half-wave, ignoring Regan, and rode off after Kal.

Regan watched them go, frowning. 'I'm going to work out what's going on with those two.'

Chloe shrugged. She didn't think they were behaving any more strangely than teenage boys normally did.

Regan gestured towards Jiao, who was still waiting by the school gate. 'Do you think that Jiao guy is a bit weird?'

'Not really,' replied Chloe.

'Keep an eye on him,' Regan replied as if Chloe had wholeheartedly agreed with her. 'Call me if you see anything and I'll put in a good word for you.'

Chloe nodded unconvincingly. 'Sure, Regan. See you later,' she said before walking quickly down the road before Regan could respond.

•

Circular Quay was still bustling with tourists and ferry-goers as Rose, Gemma, Jacob and Kymara stood on the Cahill Expressway surveying the scene below. Each shrouded in a hoodie, they scanned the area in search of the discarded walkie-talkie.

'There it is!' Kymara pointed to the bench next to the busker she had hustled that morning; clearly his time with the Infinity Group thugs was temporary, because there he stood, still in character and still attracting attention from passers-by.

Gemma shook her head. 'You had to pick the busiest place in the whole of Sydney to leave something behind?' she asked bitterly.

'I said I'm sorry,' said Kymara with a pout.

Rose, ever the planner, was scoping out the potential risks. 'If we're lucky, Infinity Group haven't found it yet. If we're unlucky, this is a trap and we're about to be busted.'

The others looked around, unsure whether the odds were even worth considering.

Rose continued. 'We're going down. Jacob, you hold the lift doors open at the bottom, okay? Gemma, jump in if I need backup.'

Gemma nodded, a little unsure.

'But Rose,' asked Kymara, 'what can I do?'

Rose sighed. Her expression made it clear Kymara was not yet forgiven. 'You can wait here. You're too good at attracting attention.'

Jacob gently patted Kymara's shoulder. 'Sorry, Ky. Going viral just isn't a skill we need right now, eh?'

As she watched her friends get in the lift, Kymara blinked back tears as she kept a bird's-eye view on the crowds below, trying to remain inconspicuous.

The lift doors opened on Circular Quay and the three teens shared a nervous glance before Rose moved towards the backpack, strolling with carefully feigned nonchalance to the bench. No-one seemed to notice as she picked up the backpack but as she turned to leave, an older woman sitting on the next bench along reached over and grabbed the strap. 'Excuse me. I don't think that is yours,' the woman said.

Rose stared at the woman, trying to remain calm. 'Yeah, it's mine.'

Clearly the woman didn't believe her, and called out to the crowd: 'This girl is taking the bag! It's not hers! She's stealing it!'

'It *is* my bag,' hissed Rose furiously. This busybody old lady was risking the whole operation!

In the distance, Jacob saw two security guards look

over in Rose's direction. Jacob motioned to Gemma to go over and help Rose, but Gemma stood rooted to the spot, terrified.

Frustrated, Jacob realised it was up to him. His leg was still sore from the injury he'd got a few days earlier when he'd met with the twins so, limping a little, he ran over to Rose and said loudly, 'Hey, you found my bag – thanks! Now we have to go.' Jacob snatched the backpack off the woman and limped quickly back to the lift, Rose following close behind him.

The woman looked suspiciously after the teenagers but decided there was no more she could do. The youth of today were rude and possibly criminal, but it wasn't her job to try to change that, was it?

Gemma had the lift door open waiting for Rose and Jacob, and she almost collapsed as the doors shut with everyone inside. 'You made it,' she said, taking a deep breath. Seeing Gemma's response made Rose and Jacob break out into giggles. Even though they were scared, it was a relief to know they were all in this together.

CHAPTER FIVE

Arriving home after school, the twins tumbled through the front door and raced upstairs. Dru grabbed the laptop out of his bag and searched for Kymara's video.

'Why is Kymara posting again? It's way too dangerous,' said Kal.

Dru nodded in agreement. 'We have to take that video down right now, before she attracts unwanted attention.' As Dru typed in the address, an alarm sounded through the laptop's speaker.

Dru was confused, 'What's happen— Oh no. Oh *no, oh no.*'

'Turn it off!' hissed Kal, just as the boys' sister, sixteen-year-old Vidya, burst into their bedroom.

Dru slammed the laptop shut and the alarm stopped.

Vidya eyed her brothers suspiciously, her dark brown eyes flashing. 'What's going on in here?'

The boys shrugged. 'Nothing,' they replied in unison.

Vidya paused for a moment, but they weren't giving anything away. 'Did one of you take my hairdryer?'

The boys looked at her in disbelief. 'No.'

'Okay, well . . . I'm watching you.' She gave them an intimidating big-sister stare before closing the door.

Dru instantly opened the laptop and the alarm started up again. Over the noise, Dru explained, 'I set up security shells around my IP, and one's been breached.'

Kal looked at his brother, clearly not understanding what he was talking about.

Dru continued with a sigh. 'Someone's monitoring activity on Kymara's account. It's probably Infinity Group. They waited for me to come back, and I walked straight into it.'

Now this made sense to Kal. 'Does this mean they know who you are?' he asked.

'Not yet,' said Dru. 'I figure we've got about two hours until they break through the rest of the security shells.'

Kal shook his head. 'Dude. What is up with you today? You keep making silly mistakes.'

Dru's shoulders slumped. 'I know. While you're becoming stronger and smarter I'm . . . losing it.'

'There must be a way to stop this. Can you delete Kymara's account?'

Dru thought about it for a second. It wasn't a bad idea. 'I can't hack into it but if I could log in as Kymara, I could delete all of it.'

'Then let's get her password.' Kal reached for the walkie-talkie, pleased he'd helped come up with a tech solution for a change. The walkie-talkie crackled to life. 'Twin one to Unlisted. Twin one to Unlisted. Come in, Unlisted.'

But there was no reply.

Dru raised an eyebrow. 'Twin one. Really?'

Kal ignored his brother's look. 'If they're not answering we'll have to go to the tunnels and get the password from Kymara.'

Dru closed the laptop and placed it on his desk. 'But I have some history homework I really should –'

Kal rolled his eyes. 'Let's go!'

Dru followed Kal down the stairs in a rush, shouting out a quick goodbye to their grandmother, Dadi, before they had to explain where they were going. Dadi was the glue that kept the Sharma family together and was generally found in the kitchen, listening to Indian radio and whipping up a delicious meal for the family. The moment the twins opened the front door, they were stopped in their tracks.

On the front step stood two people, one of which, their aunt Maya, was reaching to ring the doorbell. The other was also familiar, but for a different reason.

'Hey, you two,' said Maya, smiling, pleased to see her favourite nephews. 'I'm so glad I caught you. I believe you've met . . .' she gestured towards Jiao, standing behind her with his bags. 'Jiao Yang. At school? He'll be staying with you for the remainder of his time in Sydney.'

The twins' mouths fell open.

See you soon. All of a sudden Dru understood why Jiao had spoken those words earlier. And he felt a chill run down his spine.

•

In contrast to her grandsons' reactions to Jiao coming to stay, Dadi was thrilled to have another house guest. To prove her superior hostess skills, she went all out to provide a late afternoon feast for Jiao and the rest of the Sharmas. She rang the twins' mum and dad, Anousha and Rahul, and demanded they leave work early so they could properly welcome their house guest.

Having to stay at home and look like they were happy to have a student from China staying with them was not easy for the boys. It meant delaying getting in touch with the Unlisted, which in turn meant that the countdown to Infinity Group finding out who had accessed Kymara's account was getting closer and closer. All in all, the situation did not help the twins feel either relaxed or social as Dadi served up her smorgasbord of food.

Dadi did not hide her disappointment in the lack of effort her grandsons were making with their guest. 'Talk to your new friend,' she badgered Kal as she passed around her famous *laddus*, round Indian balls of deliciousness the boys normally devoured in seconds. But right now neither twin had much of an appetite.

'Um . . . how was your first day at Westbrook?' asked Kal, sounding like he didn't really care to know the answer.

'Good, thank you,' answered Jiao politely.

Before Dru was called upon to contribute to the lacklustre conversation, Maya made an announcement. 'I'd heard at work that Jiao's original host family had pulled out at the last minute. And I know how welcoming the Sharma family is – so, I thought it would work out well for everyone.'

Rahul smiled. 'We're happy to have you, Jiao.'

Dadi sidled up next to Jiao while offering him more laddus. 'Super happy.'

Dru started to get up from the table before Dadi stopped him. 'Where are you off to?' she asked sternly.

'Uh . . . to finish my history homework,' said Dru.

But a look from Dadi made him sit back down again. 'Plenty of time for that later. Another snack, Jiao?'

Jiao smiled. 'Thank you.'

'That's an interesting necklace,' said Dadi as she nodded towards a pendant hanging around Jiao's neck. It looked like a small glass vial with something in it. 'Is it something Chinese?' she added as she reached out to touch it.

Jiao moved away from her touch and put his hand up protectively to cover the pendant. As the family shared curious glances Jiao once again smiled politely. 'Ah, thank you,' he said.

Dru noted he did not answer her question directly.

'And these sweets are delicious,' Jiao added, popping another one into his mouth, smiling while he chewed.

'I'm so glad you like them,' said Dadi, charmed by her guest.

Maya spoke to the twins quietly while the rest of the family chatted. 'I need to check Jacob's leg tomorrow. To make sure the infection's gone.'

The boys had asked for their bua's help when Jacob's cut got infected, but that was before they knew she was about to start working for the Global Child Initiative. She looked at the twins' stony expressions and added: 'It's for his own good, boys.'

The boys squirmed. 'Yes, Bua,' replied Dru reluctantly, knowing that there was no way he and Kal would let Jacob anywhere near Maya's work.

After three or four more courses of Dadi's finest mouth-watering baking, Maya stood up to leave.

'You're in good hands here, Jiao,' she said, giving the boy's shoulder a reassuring squeeze. 'My mother is the best hostess in the neighbourhood. But now I have to head back to the office to finish up some lab work.'

Dadi smiled and gave her daughter a big hug. 'Don't work too hard, darling.'

After the boys' aunt had left, Dru and Kal were
tasked with cleaning up the kitchen. They were hoping
for a moment alone to work out how they were going
to delete Kymara's account and warn Jacob, but Jiao
wouldn't leave their side.

'Oh, please, Jiao, no chores,' said Dadi when he
offered to help tidy up. 'You're our guest.'

Kal agreed wholeheartedly. 'Yeah, go into the other
room. Sit and relax.'

'Or you could go outside. Enjoy the sunshine,'
added Dru hopefully.

Jiao protested as he started to stack plates. 'Thank
you, but I wish to show gratitude for your hospitality.'

Dadi beamed, obviously very impressed with this
lovely guest.

Dru whispered to Kal, 'We're running out of time
to delete that account! I've got an idea.'

Jiao leaned closer to the brothers, but he couldn't
quite catch what they were saying.

Kal whispered back. 'Nah, bro, we won't survive
another one of your ideas. Follow my lead.' Kal turned

to Dadi. 'Hey, Dadi. We're doing yoga at school tomorrow. It'll be great to introduce Jiao to a bit of our culture.'

Dadi looked horrified. 'What? Western yoga?! No, no, this will not do. Jiao, come with me.'

She grabbed Jiao's hand and they left the kitchen and moved through the open doorway into the lounge room.

'I have eaten a lot of your nice food,' said Jiao pleasantly as he followed. 'Perhaps now is not the time for yoga?' With his last words he looked behind at the boys with a flash of frustration and caught them giving each other a celebratory high-five. As they continued washing dishes they could hear as Dadi schooled Jiao in 'true' – i.e. Indian – yoga.

'The West took an ancient Indian spiritual practice and reduced it to calisthenics,' Dadi said bitterly. 'The true purpose of yoga is not tight buttocks. It is *moksha* – a state of total enlightenment.'

Dru and Kal glanced into the lounge room and saw Jiao reluctantly sit down, cross-legged, as Dadi continued her lecture. He tried to stand up. 'It's very kind of you to show me, but –'

Dadi stopped him in his tracks. 'Hush now. Eyes closed. Hands together.'

Jiao did as he was told, and Dru and Kal shared a conspiratorial smile.

'*Real* yoga is about *hours* of long meditation.'

Jiao opened an eye. 'Hours?' he questioned unhappily.

Dadi started humming. '*Ommm, ommm.*'

Jiao remained seated, frowning. If he had dared to open his eyes he would have seen Dru and Kal quietly race upstairs to their bedroom, trying to muffle their laughter.

Jiao had well and truly lost this round.

CHAPTER SIX

The twins sat on Dru's bed with the laptop open. The alarm was still beeping and they were seriously running out of time. Dru lowered the volume and examined his security systems. 'They got through my security shells faster than I thought. They could break through any minute.'

Kal grabbed the walkie-talkie. 'Twin one to Unlisted. Come in, Unlisted!' They waited for a response before a crackle announced someone was on the other end.

'Unlisted here. Over.'

'Rose, finally! It's Kal. Where have you been?'

'Hi Kal. It's a long story, but we're back in the tunnels now. What's up?'

Kal handed the walkie-talkie to Dru, who wasted no time being polite. 'Dru here. Infinity Group is about to trace us through Kymara's account, and to avoid that we need to delete the account now. What's Kymara's password?' he said in one long breath.

'What?' Kymara's voice came over the line. 'You can't delete my account! It's my life.'

Kal grabbed the walkie-talkie back from Dru. 'We're running out of time, Kymara. You're all in danger!'

•

Kymara paced around the hide-out, her distress clear to her new friends.

Gemma reached for Kymara's hand. 'You have to give them the password.'

'But what about the video I posted today? People will be replying,' said Kymara, desperate. 'And my post might be all they have.'

Rose rolled her eyes. 'I can't believe you're still talking about that silly video, after all the danger it put us in. Your gaming videos aren't important anymore,' she finished harshly.

But Kymara wasn't going to give up without a fight. She grabbed the walkie-talkie. 'Okay, Kal, Dru. I'll give you the password on one condition. Please watch the video first and then read the comments before deleting my account. And come and meet us at Observatory Hill afterwards. Let me know what was said.'

Back in the boys' bedroom, Dru and Kal looked at each other, frustrated. With Jiao staying in the house, how could they go anywhere? 'We can't get away right now.'

'Please,' Kymara begged. 'I need to know if it worked.'

There was a moment of silence before Dru spoke. 'Okay. I promise.'

Kymara sighed. 'Thanks. My password is Monkeyface. Capital M, zero for O.'

•

With the alarm still blaring, Dru flipped to the login screen. He typed in the password and it took him to the account control panel. 'I'm in!'

'Twin one, over and out,' said Kal as he switched off the walkie-talkie.

Dru was scanning the info on the site.

'Delete it now,' said Kal.

Dru shook his head. He was determined to fulfil his promise to Kymara. He brought up the video and played it, fast-forwarding through the footage. 'I want your *letters* to the editor, so hit me up in the comments and let me know I'm not the only *Steve* in *Zomville*. Peace and love!'

Dru freeze-framed on Kymara with the letters *SSP?* visible on her finger. 'SSP. Of course,' he nodded, impressed. 'Clever.' He scrolled down the comments. 'Oh my gosh. There are fifteen thousand comments. I can't read all those. Unless . . .' Dru opened a new window and started coding.

'Dru! We don't have time for whatever you're doing!' Kal whisper-shouted.

Dru was scrambling to get the program running. He pressed enter and run, just as Kal reached over, grabbed the mouse and hit DELETE ACCOUNT.

'Not yet!' yelled Dru.

But the screen now said ACCOUNT DELETED. 'You've been wrong about every single thing today,' Kal reminded his brother. 'We can't take any more risks.' Kal closed the laptop, and, over Dru's protests, put it and the walkie-talkie in his bag. 'We should go now while Jiao's distracted.'

Dru finally, reluctantly agreed but was still annoyed by Kal's actions. He followed his brother down the stairs and they crept out the front door, this time without anyone stopping them.

•

Outside the twins' home, Regan loitered on the street. She recorded a video of herself on her phone, whispering. 'Year Leader's log. Five-thirty p.m. Outside Sharma house, following tip-off from Chloe. Jiao believed to be inside. What's he doing there?'

Regan was startled by a noise nearby and ducked behind a bush. She flipped her screen around and filmed the twins walking down the side of their house onto the driveway, where their bikes were lying. Dru went to pick his bike up but saw that the front wheel was seriously bent out of shape. The family car in the driveway had magnetic L plates next to the number plate.

'Oh my god, Vidya!' he cried, then turned to his brother. 'Look how she ended her driving lesson – she ran over my bike! Can today get *any* worse?'

Dru looked in disbelief as Kal grabbed the mangled front wheel and bent it back into shape as if it were Play-Doh. 'Fixed,' he said with a grin, returning to his own bike and jumping on it.

As the boys rode away, Regan moved out from behind the bush and ended the video. She grabbed her bike and took off after them.

•

At Observatory Hill the four Unlisted were hidden behind a picnic shelter, waiting.

The boys rode over to them. The boys could see the strain on their faces, and the dark circles under their eyes. Even before they'd got off their bikes, Kymara was badgering them to tell her what had happened.

'So? Were there any comments? Did you read them?'

Kal shook his head. 'There was no time. We had to delete the account or we would have been discovered.'

Kymara turned to Dru, her devastation all over her face. 'But . . . you promised.'

Dru looked guilty. 'I captured what I could . . .' He pulled out his laptop, and started typing.

Kymara looked over his shoulder at the results.

'I got sixteen,' said Dru with a shrug. 'It's actually better than I suspected.'

Kymara was wide-eyed. 'Oh my god – sixteen!'

Jacob looked at Dru and Kymara, waiting for an explanation. 'Is somebody gonna tell the rest of us what sixteen means?'

Dru explained. 'When Kymara said "Steve" and "Zomville", I knew she was talking Minecraft. And the letters she showed – "SSP" – refer to Survival Single

Player. She was asking her followers if she was alone. All I had to do was search the comments for "SMP".'

Kymara was nodding. 'Exactly. Survival Multi-Player.'

Dru looked at Kymara. 'Genius idea!'

'Thanks!' said Kymara, chuffed. After the day Kymara had had trying to defend her actions to everyone, it felt pretty good to know that someone understood what she'd done and why.

The others were still in the dark about what was really going on, though. 'Guys! You have to loop us in here,' said Rose. 'Speak in a language we all understand.'

Kymara turned the laptop towards the others. On the screen was a list of usernames. 'These are some of the kids across Australia who responded to my call-out,' she explained. 'They're all like us. Unlisted.'

Rose, Gemma and Jacob stared at the screen as Kymara's words sank in.

'See,' she added, 'we're not alone.'

•

Kymara was right in more ways than one. A short

distance away, Regan leant her bike against a tree and approached the picnic area. She could see that Kal and Dru were talking to some kids, but she wasn't close enough to make out who they were. She moved closer, thrilled that she was about to uncover in exactly what way the Sharma twins were being shady, and to be proved right in her suspicions about them. She focused on the kids the twins had met here. They didn't look like they were from Westbrook High, but she was still too far away to be sure.

Just as she was about to shout out and tell them they'd been busted, out of nowhere – *WHUMP!* – a figure jumped down from a tree directly in front of her. Startled, Regan staggered, falling backwards and hitting her head on a tree root as she fell to the ground.

•

Hearing a tussle nearby, Dru and Kal, along with the Unlisted, turned suddenly to see Regan lying on the ground and Jiao Yang standing over her.

'Who's that?' asked Jacob.

'What happened?' asked Rose.

'Does she need our help?' asked Gemma.

'Run!' shouted Kal, deciding now was not the time to get into complicated explanations.

Kymara was happy to take Kal's advice. 'Let's go!'

As Jiao started walking towards them, the kids scattered, racing in every direction.

CHAPTER SEVEN

Dru ducked behind a tree to catch his breath. After a moment, he stepped out to try to find Kal – but instead of his twin brother, it was Jiao who appeared right in front of him.

'Please, Dru,' said Jiao. 'I need your help.'

This was the last thing that Dru expected to come out of Jiao's mouth. He was so surprised he didn't object as Jiao walked with him over to a semi-conscious Regan, explaining that from the moment he stepped into the classroom he had recognised that Dru was different to the other students.

When Dru, his heart racing, started to disagree, Jiao held up his hand to silence him. 'I recognised you because you and I are the same.'

'What do you mean?' asked Dru, his heart hammering in his chest.

'The implant,' said Jiao. 'You don't have one, do you?'

Dru stared at Jiao, a thousand thoughts racing through his mind but none forming on his lips.

'I don't either,' said Jiao simply.

Dru didn't know if he believed what Jiao was saying, but right now they had to deal with the fact that Regan was regaining consciousness. Jiao said to Dru, 'You should hide. I can handle Regan.' Dru wasn't sure this was true, but he didn't have a better plan. He nodded his head in agreement and hid out of sight.

Jiao crouched beside Regan, who started to moan then put her hand to her head. She looked up at Jiao. 'What happened?'

Jiao patted her hand. 'You're okay. I'm not going to tell anyone.'

Regan didn't register what Jiao had said. 'My head. Ow. Someone jumped out in front of me . . .'

Jiao smiled encouragingly at Regan. 'Excellent idea. Tell them someone scared you. You didn't just pass out.' He went to help her up but she shrugged him off.

'I didn't just pass out,' she said, confused.

He nodded. 'Great. That's your story. Because if they find out you're weak, they'll replace you as Year Leader.'

Regan looked horrified. 'But – I –' she broke off, speechless.

Jiao shifted his attention to the park. 'Did you see where the other kids went?'

Regan's eyes narrowed, as if things were slowly becoming clearer in her mind. 'No. And what are *you* doing here?'

'I was following Kal and Dru, like you. I thought they were acting suspiciously and I wanted to find out why. They ran away when you fainted, though, and I didn't find out anything. Don't worry – your secret's safe with me.'

Regan's facial expression told Jiao she didn't entirely

believe him, but nor did she trust her own memory right now. 'Thanks, Jiao,' she said finally.

Jiao patted her back. 'I'll keep an eye on the Sharma twins. Now that I'm staying with them, it will be easy.'

Hidden in the bushes nearby, Dru watched in awe of Jiao's ability to smoothly manipulate Regan. He was a natural.

He still had no idea what to make of Jiao, but it was disaster averted . . . for now.

•

Dru and Jiao barely made it home in time for dinner. Kal was already back but the twins didn't get a chance to talk and then it was time for bed. Dadi hovered around them, making sure Jiao had absolutely everything he needed and making it impossible to discuss what had gone on at Observatory Hill. After she'd come in and checked for the third time that Jiao had enough blankets, all three boys were so exhausted they fell asleep almost immediately.

It wasn't until the next morning that Dru had a

chance to fill Kal in on what had happened after he'd run away from the park. Kal was freshly showered and dressed for school, while Dru was still in pyjamas.

There was a mattress on the floor near Dru's bed, and Jiao's clothes spilled out from a suitcase nearby.

'Why are you being so stubborn? asked Dru.

'Isn't it obvious? I don't trust him,' replied his brother.

Dru sighed. He'd explained the situation to Kal several times but he still wouldn't listen to sense. 'Jiao doesn't have an implant. He's pretending. Like me. He saved us all from Regan.'

Kal scoffed. 'Or maybe they're working together.'

'If you had seen Jiao with Regan yesterday, you'd believe he's on our side, but you didn't stick around at Observatory Hill long enough.'

Kal puffed up in indignation, but before he could reply, Dadi bustled into the room and immediately frowned at Dru. 'Why aren't you dressed for school, wombat?'

'Jiao's in the shower,' replied Dru.

'Well, quick sticks. There's a special breakfast waiting downstairs,' she said as she headed out of the room.

Moments later Jiao walked into the bedroom, showered and wearing school clothes with the shirt unbuttoned. He was wearing his necklace, but the pendant was missing.

Dru headed to the bathroom, reluctantly leaving Jiao and Kal alone.

Jiao burrowed through his suitcase, obviously searching for something.

Kal eyed him suspiciously. 'What are you up to?'

'The pendant from my necklace. Have you seen it?'

'Why should I help you?'

Jiao paused and watched Kal carefully. He glanced at the open bedroom door before he spoke quietly. 'Because the pendant holds my implant.'

Kal sat back in surprise. 'You've been carrying it with you?'

Jiao closed the bedroom door and sat opposite Kal. In China, he explained, when the compulsory dental checks had taken place, his implant had fallen out of his mouth soon afterwards, clearly not inserted properly. He immediately realised something was wrong, and he was smart enough to know that he needed to pretend he was in the same position as his school friends, so he kept the implant close. As he saw the changes in his fellow students he became more and more scared that he would be found out. At the same time, he was horrified by what he was seeing, and when the opportunity came up for a select group of students to go to Sydney, Australia, as exchange students, he jumped at the chance to find out more about what was happening elsewhere.

When Dru came out of the shower and back into the room fearing the worst, he was surprised to find Kal and Jiao chatting like old friends.

'You believe him now, do you?' Dru asked Kal. Then he turned to Jiao. 'What are you looking for?'

'My pendant. With my implant in it.' Jiao was still shuffling through his suitcase, then he looked up suddenly, as a thought struck him. 'I think I know where it might be.'

'Where?' asked Kal.

Jiao looked frightened. 'It must have fallen off in the park yesterday, when I jumped in front of Regan.'

The three boys looked at each other but didn't have time to speak as they heard Dadi's voice call from downstairs: 'Breakfast now, wombats. Before it gets cold!'

Jiao frowned. 'Wombats? What does your dadi mean? Aren't wombats Australian marsupials?'

Dru and Kal shared a smile. 'Yes, and it's also our nickname.'

Jiao nodded. 'Oh, I see.' But he didn't really.

•

Sitting in the tunnels, Rose and the others could only wish they had a dadi to cook them a delicious Indian breakfast. Instead, they were forcing down yesterday's stale leftovers: the last few pieces of bread discarded beside the Botanic Gardens duck pond, and the tasteless but filling white rice from a discarded plastic container. Gemma had scrounged a couple of apples left behind after a toddler threw a tantrum and had to be dragged away by his flustered mother.

They each took a bite of the last apple and passed it around.

'My food-hygiene habits have slipped,' said Jacob as he took a bite. 'I would never have shared an apple with anyone other than my own family.'

Gemma smiled. 'My best friend Sasha and I used to take turns sucking the apple core to get every last bit of juice out of it.'

Kymara grimaced at Gemma's admission but took a bite of the apple.

Gemma continued. 'Sasha has a huge Granny Smith tree in her backyard. They're sour and delicious.'

Rose wasn't taking part in the conversation. She was busy trying to get through to the Sharmas on the walkie-talkie. When there was finally a response, she launched straight in. 'What happened last night?

Who were those two kids spying on us? Are you okay? Twin one, are you there, twin one?'

•

After eating an enormous breakfast, the three boys didn't have time to take a detour to the park before school, but they had smuggled the walkie-talkie out in Dru's backpack, and when Rose's voice came through, they moved to a quiet place in the schoolyard.

Dru whispered into the handheld device. 'The boy you saw is called Jiao. He's staying with us. He's from China. And Regan is a girl from school who's acting like a spy for Infinity Group. Jiao was protecting us from Regan last night. But he dropped his pendant in the park and we need you to go find it.'

Rose's response wasn't what he was hoping for: laughter. 'That's a big risk to take for jewellery.'

'Rose. Jiao's implant is inside the pendant. It fell out just after his dental check-up – they did them in China too. Anyway, he's unlisted, like us, and we need to help him stay that way. It's a glass vial with a metal base.'

There was silence at the other end.

Then Jacob's voice could be heard. 'China, did you say?'

Dru nodded, even though he knew the Unlisted couldn't see them. 'I know what you're thinking. And you're right. It's bigger than we thought. Whatever Infinity Group is doing to us, it's happening to kids in other countries too.'

The school bell rang. Kal gestured to Dru that they had to head into class. 'Rose, we have to go. Please help Jiao. He's on our side. Please!'

CHAPTER EIGHT

Rose looked anxiously at the others as the walkie-talkie crackled and fell silent. They stared back in disbelief.

Jacob was the first to speak. 'They want us to search the whole park? In broad daylight?'

Kymara was thinking through the implications. 'Even if we do find it, that would mean we'd have an implant and Infinity Group could track us.'

'It's a huge risk,' agreed Jacob.

Rose frowned. 'I don't think the twins would risk our safety if it wasn't important.'

Kymara wasn't convinced. 'What makes this one

kid so important when we know there are sixteen others – at least – out there who've made contact online? Why aren't we looking for *them*?'

Rose responded firmly: 'Because we can help Jiao *right now.*' They looked at each other, conflicted.

'Wait a minute . . .' Gemma moved over to a pile of junk in the corner of their hide-out. She rummaged through it, discarding scrap metal and a few pieces of clothing and several hi-vis vests, until she stopped. 'Ta-da!' she said triumphantly as she held up an old-looking metal detector.

A huge smile crossed Rose's face. 'Nice work, Gemms.'

•

Gemma's discovery gave their day a purpose, and they set out for Observatory Hill once again. As with their trip to Circular Quay it was broad daylight, but this time they didn't just rely on their hoodies to avoid attracting attention; they knew they had to be clever. So, when they arrived, the four of them wore hi-vis vests. It was counterintuitive, but they agreed that looking conspicuous might make them look less suspicious. Hiding in plain sight.

Kymara was still identifiable to her fans, so she also wore a large floppy hat. If anyone paid too close attention to their equipment, they would have realised it was all held together with duct tape, but from a distance it looked almost like proper surveying equipment.

Jacob and Rose stood at one end with the pretend theodolite, which was made from three old broom handles with an old video camera perched on top of the tripod. Kymara positioned herself a distance away with a fake marker post.

Gemma moved from Kymara towards Jacob and Rose, holding the metal detector and scanning the ground as she walked.

Jacob was looking around and suddenly whispered, 'Someone's coming.' He nodded towards a man in a suit walking through the park, talking on his phone.

Rose gave him a confident smile. 'Relax. Act like you're supposed to be here. No-one is going to suspect anything.' She put a reassuring arm on his shoulder. 'Everyone knows that kids on the run don't wear hi-vis vests out in public.'

Jacob nodded a little more confidently, as Gemma moved the metal detector slowly across the ground.

•

At Westbrook High School, Mr Park watched on, resigned, as the class filed out of the school building and into the quadrangle, all crooked lines and loitering students. 'Have a good time, kids. Maybe tomorrow we'll get around to actually having a maths lesson,' he said sarcastically. The teacher turned and walked back into the school building.

A moment later all the students' movements became robotic. Kal, who had been walking with Dru and Jiao, sped up and moved away from them.

Regan moved to the head of the group and began calling out instructions in a monotone. 'Neat lines. No talking.'

Dru and Jiao looked at each other, alarmed. They

did their best to look as though they were responding to the same instructions as the other students.

Dru turned to Kal. 'What are we doing?'

Kal didn't answer.

'Dru, sh,' interjected Jiao. 'Don't talk, just follow.'

The students were now in neat lines. Dru and Jiao stood in the back row trying not to look out of place as Miss Biggs walked to the front of the group, studying the students.

Then, within moments, all the kids were back to their normal selves, laughing and talking.

Miss Biggs smiled. 'Congratulations, students. You've made great progress – and you deserve a reward. In a moment, a bus will arrive to take you to the Global Child Initiative headquarters.'

Dru turned to Kal, who was looking around as if nothing had just happened. 'We can't go to headquarters! We'll get busted for sure.'

Jiao looked ashen. 'As long as you two stick together, you might get away with it. But without my implant, I don't stand a chance.'

Dru immediately understood the threat to Jiao. He grabbed Kal by the shoulder and started heading back towards the school.

Regan shouted after them, 'Oi, Sharmas! Back in line.'

Dru kept moving, pushing Kal ahead of him. He shouted back to Regan, 'Kal gets motion sickness.'

Kal added, 'If I go on that bus without Dadi's ginger pills, things will get ugly. I have some in my locker.'

Regan didn't trust them. 'I'll go with you, then.'

Jiao stepped next to Regan and said quietly, 'You shouldn't overdo it, given what happened last night. I'll supervise.' He followed after Dru and Kal before Regan could object.

Regan watched the three boys leave, her eyes narrowing with suspicion.

•

Back at Observatory Hill, Gemma reached Rose and Jacob at the end of another sweep of the ground. Still no sign of Jiao's pendant.

Up ahead, a short distance from the other kids, Kymara was positioned as group lookout.

'The battery's almost out of juice,' Gemma said, holding up the old metal detector. The light on top of the machine was flashing a weaker and weaker signal.

'We only have six square metres left to check,' responded Rose.

Kymara watched with growing alarm as, on the edge of the park, a black Infinity Group van pulled up. Two security guards stepped out of the van and began to walk up the path in the direction of the kids.

Kymara scurried over to her friends. 'Infinity Group. Coming this way. Time to go.'

Rose turned to Gemma and Kymara. 'You have to get Jacob back to the tunnels, *now*.' Rose grabbed the metal detector from Gemma.

Jacob protested but his leg was still sore and he moved slowly.

'I'll just do this last patch,' explained Rose.

Jacob and Gemma moved off, but Kymara wasn't happy. 'We've got to go. Now. All of us.'

She quickly packed up the fake surveying equipment, stowing it under a bush.

As Rose scanned the last section of the park the detector gave a half-hearted beep as Rose passed it over some bark underneath a tree. She crouched down and started feeling around for the pendant.

The security guards were getting closer to where the girls were searching. But Rose knew she was close and couldn't give up now.

Kymara knelt beside her, looking. Then Rose's finger found something other than loose bark. She showed it to Kymara silently and the two girls got up and bolted behind a tree. A moment later the Infinity Group security guards walked along the path closest to the tree. One of the guards cast a quick glance at the tree, but continued walking. As soon as they'd passed, Kymara and Rose slipped away in the opposite direction, terrified by their near miss but thrilled they had successfully found Jiao's missing pendant.

CHAPTER **NINE**

Most of the Westbrook High students had now moved out to the carpark where the bus was waiting to transport them.

Jiao, Kal and Dru returned to the empty quadrangle. They quickly huddled unobserved as Dru tried the walkie-talkie.

Rose answered immediately. 'We found it!'

Jiao was hugely relieved. 'Thank you,' he said into the walkie-talkie.

'Great,' added Dru. 'Now, we're being taken on a school trip to Global Child Initiative headquarters in the city. Do you know where that is?'

The walkie-talkie crackled. 'Yeah, it's the big building on Hunter Street,' replied Rose. 'Not far from Observatory Hill.'

'Okay. Good,' answered Dru. 'Because Jiao needs the pendant in case they scan us on the way in. Could you bring it to us?'

Before they could hear Rose's answer, Regan walked into the quadrangle, looking for them. 'Come on, you three! On the bus now! Miss Biggs is waiting.'

Dru looked at Kal and Jiao, worried. Kal opened his backpack for Dru to put the walkie-talkie in, and when he saw the tiffin and lassi containers in there he had an idea.

•

The bush pulled into the carpark and the twins looked out the window at the imposing building, worried about what would happen if they managed to even get inside the Global Child Initiative headquarters.

The students got off the bus and Kal waited until

last before disembarking. He looked like he was about to be sick and, hands over his mouth, he ran to a bush and proceeded to fake vomit a concoction made from Dadi's breakfast mixed with lassi and orange juice. It looked disgusting, and the class groaned and moved as far away from Kal as possible.

Regan walked over to Jiao, furious, as though this were his fault. 'What happened to the ginger pills?'

She stared at Jiao, but Jiao merely shrugged.

Kal fake vomited a bit more, close to Regan, and she leapt back in horror. 'That's foul.'

Miss Biggs surveyed the scene. 'That's enough, class. Dru, can you please help your brother?'

Dru and Jiao led Kal, who kept his hands over his mouth, away from the bush, towards a hedge a distance away from the building entrance.

Regan watched as the other students headed towards the building, then looked back at Dru, Jiao and Kal, who was making loud retching noises. She looked away in disgust.

Up close, Jiao held the tiffin containing the orange

juice, lassi and food concoction, pouring it out while the three boys talked.

Dru looked around. 'They're heading to the entrance of the building.'

Jiao was tipping the last bits of Dadi's precious lunch out of the containers. 'We're almost out of vomit.'

Kal looked at the food on the ground. 'Dadi would never forgive us if she saw what we'd done with her lunch.'

'We can never tell her this hap—'

Dru's sentence was cut short by a hissing noise coming from the carpark. '*Psst*. Hey, Kal, Dru.'

The three boys turned to see Rose and Kymara crouched out of sight.

'Dru! Kal! Jiao!' Regan was refusing to leave the boys alone. She started marching in their direction.

Dru removed a printout from his bag and handed it to Kal. 'Give this to Kymara. We'll cover for you.'

Kal took the printout and headed towards Kymara and Rose, holding his hand to his middle as if he were about to erupt again.

Jiao and Dru walked up to Regan, stopping her progress. 'It's under control, Regan,' said Jiao. He then pushed Dru and said rudely, 'You. Pick up the pace.'

'Where's Kal gone?' asked Regan.

'He needed to use the bathroom,' a quick-thinking Dru responded. 'Well, not actually a bathroom, just the closest bush . . .' he trailed off, leaving the rest to Regan's imagination.

'*Ew.* Boys are *so* gross!' she said as she walked Dru and Jiao back to the building.

'Thanks for this,' said Kal gratefully as he reached Rose and Kymara. 'You might just have saved Jiao's life.' Rose peered at the small object inside the vial and shuddered as she handed it over. 'How can something so tiny have already had such an impact on our lives?' she said as Kal looked closely at the pendant.

'Yep, tiny but evil.' Kal handed the printout to Kymara. 'Dru wanted you to have this.'

Kymara looked down at the sheet, a slow smile spreading across her face. 'The usernames of the sixteen unlisted kids who deciphered my code.' She looked at

Rose. 'Now we have to find a way to make contact with them.'

'See what you can find out about what's going on in there,' Rose said to Kal, gesturing towards the mirrored building.

'I'll do my best,' he said, then raced off to join the rest of his class.

At the entrance, Regan, Jiao and Dru were waiting in a queue. Inside the front glass doors was a security officer and a man in a white lab coat, who was using a device to scan students as they passed through a metal detector on their way into the building.

Dru and Jiao were at the back of the line, trying not to look as nervous as they felt. Dru muttered under his breath. 'Hurry up, Kal. Hurry up, Kal.' He and Jiao had so much to lose if they were found out.

Regan glanced back at them regularly; clearly she knew that something was going on, but she had no idea what. Suddenly she called out to Jiao: 'You can go next.' She pushed Jiao forward, virtually frogmarching him to the front of the queue, where Miss Biggs was supervising the security check. The exchange student desperately looked around for Kal to make a magical appearance, but there was no sign of him.

Dru thought fast. He sidled up to Miss Biggs and surreptitiously slipped something into her jacket pocket.

When Miss Biggs stepped near the metal detector a moment later, an alarm sounded. The man in the lab coat frowned.

The students made a collective '*oooh*' noise. What had Miss Biggs done wrong? 'All right, all right,' she said, clearly not appreciating the attention. 'Calm down, students.'

'Anything in your pockets, ma'am?' asked the man in the lab coat.

Miss Biggs shook her head no, but then she checked and pulled out some loose change. 'Oh. Apart from these coins. How did they get in there?'

The man in the lab coat rolled his eyes at the teacher's inability to follow simple instructions. He took the coins from Miss Biggs as he gestured for her to be scanned.

By this time Kal had finally reached the building

entrance. He caught Dru's eye and nodded, holding up a clenched fist.

As Miss Biggs finally made it successfully through the scanner, the surrounding students cheered – at exactly the same time as Kal dropped the pendant into Jiao's hand.

Jiao confidently entered the building a second later. Everything was as it should be.

Regan glanced at Jiao, and then back at Dru and Kal. She wasn't sure what had just happened, but she knew these three boys were playing games. And she didn't like it!

Kal and Dru were scanned through the entrance together, the man in the white lab coat not noticing anything unusual.

Regan, however, noticed Jiao adjusting the collar of his shirt. She walked over to him. 'I'm watching you,' she said menacingly.

Jiao stared at Regan, expressionless, saying nothing. He was wearing the necklace with the pendant once more.

CHAPTER TEN

Further inside the headquarters, the students were gathered in a large foyer in one big group. Jiao, Regan and Tim stood in front of the year group.

Miss Biggs addressed the students. 'All right, class. It's time to get game ready.'

She gestured for Chloe to come up to her. 'The challenge I'm about to announce is a physical one, so if you have any jewellery, please pass it to Chloe for safe-keeping. You can collect it again at the end, of course.' Miss Biggs handed Chloe a box, and Chloe started walking among the students, collecting bracelets, rings and necklaces as she went.

The man in the lab coat joined Miss Biggs, staring closely at the assembled children.

'This is Dr Wenders from the Global Child Initiative, and he'll be watching your performance closely,' explained Miss Biggs.

The twins' eyes widened as they saw their aunt walk briskly over to the group and stand next to Dr Wenders. She saw her nephews in the crowd and gave them a smile.

'Some of you may know Dr Sharma,' said Dr Wenders. 'As a health precaution, she will conduct a quick check-up on all of you before we get started. Don't worry. It's purely routine.'

Dru and Kal exchanged a wary glance. What were they really measuring?

The twins' aunt used a finger clamp to test the students' blood pressure. The children didn't seem affected by the finger clamping, and Maya moved quickly among the students, testing and moving on to the next student efficiently.

Miss Biggs looked at Kal closely. 'I hope you're over

your motion sickness now, Kalpen,' she said sternly.

Kal gave a weak smile. 'Feeling much better now, thanks.'

Miss Biggs then instructed the three leaders – Tim, Regan and Jiao – to choose teams as she explained the rules. 'Each team will go on a scavenger hunt. But this is no normal scavenger hunt – this will test your team's intelligence and your ability to work together to solve complex problems. If you complete the first test successfully, your team will be given a unique map. You will then follow that map, completing a variety of tasks that will earn you the ability to retrieve certain items along the way. It is vitally important that you don't let a weak link drag your team down.'

Dru was frowning. He turned to Kal. 'It sounds like we're going to be rats in a lab experiment.'

Kal whispered to Dru. 'Rose said we should find out anything we can about whatever program they're running while we're here.'

Dru nodded. He'd already come to the same conclusion.

'Kalpen, Drupad, please concentrate on the rules or you'll be the ones who let your team down,' ordered Miss Biggs as she glared at the whispering twins.

'Yes, Miss Biggs,' said Kal and Dru in unison.

'Kal!' Jiao called, and Kal stepped forward to join Jiao's team. Regan then called Dru to her team. Dru rolled his eyes. That girl was a constant menace.

Miss Biggs gave each of the leaders a zipped bag. 'The first team back with all their found items wins.'

The leaders continued to pick their teams as Maya reached Kal. She used the finger clamp just as she had on the other students but under her breath she asked, 'Since when do you get motion sick, Kal?'

Kal shrugged noncommittally and Maya narrowed her eyes but said nothing further. She moved on to the next student and Kal felt relieved he hadn't had to explain himself.

Miss Biggs stepped closer to the three team leaders once they'd chosen six students each. 'This will be a leadership test for the three of you.'

Regan stood taller, instantly determined to be the

best leader. She glared at her opponents, anxious to begin the test.

Chloe moved to Jiao, and held up the jewellery box in front of him. Jiao didn't move. Chloe prompted him. 'Your necklace, Jiao?'

Jiao stared at her defiantly and replied, 'No.'

'Your jewellery,' she said slowly, in case he hadn't understood her English. 'You need to take it off.'

Jiao shook his head.

Chloe remained firm. 'But it's the rule.'

'I never take it off,' Jiao replied. 'My mother gave it to me.'

Regan walked over, suddenly interested in Jiao's pendant. 'Pretty,' she said. 'Can I have a look?' She went to touch the necklace, but Jiao batted Regan's hand away from the necklace and shook her hand instead. 'May the best team win,' he said.

Regan glared at him briefly but then she held her head high and walked back to her team, even more determined to beat Jiao and Tim.

•

Once the three teams had been shown to three different starting areas, the scavenger hunt could begin in earnest. Each team waited as a countdown began over a loudspeaker. 'Three, two, one – and BEGIN!' the disembodied voice called out.

A door opened and Jiao's team burst through, running down a corridor before they came across a digitised screen mounted on a plinth. Jiao touched the screen, and three buttons lit up. A digital clock began a three-minute countdown. 'What do we have to do here?' asked one of the teammates.

Jiao looked closer, thinking fast. 'I think it is a test of reflexes. We have to hit the buttons as they light up.' He realised that without a working implant, he was not the best person for the job. 'We'll need our fastest people. Kal, Maxine and Vincent, each of you focus on one light each.'

The three kids chosen by Jiao stood before the screen, each focused on hitting their button every time it lit up. After fifteen seconds, a drawer opened in the plinth. Success. The three were congratulated by the rest of their teammates.

Jiao removed a tablet from the drawer. Pressing the 'on' button, a map appeared on the screen. It looked like a three-dimensional blueprint of the building.

'Got it, well done.' He looked at the map. 'Okay, everybody. Follow me.'

They ran down the corridor.

•

After Regan's team had successfully completed their first task, they raced through a door and down a flight of stairs to arrive at a screen mounted on a plinth. Regan was all business. 'Okay, I want you to be faster with this activity than you were with the last one.'

None of the team seemed thrilled to be bossed around by Regan, but they knew from experience that it was better to just go along with it.

Dru touched the screen and a question appeared, positioned above a keypad. A digital clock began a three-minute countdown as Dru read out loud, 'Type the number that does not belong in the sequence: two, three, six, seven, eight, fourteen, fifteen . . .'

Regan was impatient. She wasn't particularly interested in solving the problem herself – she was already thinking about winning and receiving praise from Miss Biggs about how great a leader she was. 'Just hurry up and answer it. We're losing time.'

Dru was nervous and hesitated.

Regan shouted, 'Slide in the correct numbers!'

Dru didn't like being shouted at. He couldn't concentrate, and in a panic he moved in the closest number. There was a buzzing sound and the screen flashed with the words *'Incorrect Answer'*.

Chloe looked at Dru, puzzled. 'Why did you get it wrong?'

Dru felt increasingly anxious. He knew he was surrounded by a team of kids with newly enhanced intelligence. 'Regan rushed me.'

Regan gave Dru a filthy look. 'Good one, Sharma. Now the drawer is locked for five minutes. You stay here and enter the right answer when you next get the chance. We're gonna keep moving.'

Regan and the rest of the team rushed off, following the map.

Dru hadn't meant to get the number wrong, but he now realised that his mistake had given him the opportunity he wanted. He was by himself and could try to find out exactly what the Global Child Initiative, run by Infinity Group, was doing. He waited until the rest of his group were out of sight, then walked to a nearby door, which led to another corridor. He was about to step out when several of Jiao's team members suddenly ran by; one carried a bag while another held a torch.

Dru hid back behind the door as the kids sped past. 'Kal!' he hissed as he saw his brother coming. 'Wait up!'

'Regan left me to complete the second test,' explained Dru when Kal stopped, the rest of the team now far ahead.

Kal smiled. 'Well, she won't get far with the next challenge without the torch in the plinth.'

Dru wasn't worried about the scavenger hunt. He held out his glasses to Kal. 'This might be my only chance to see what kind of network they're using. You have to pretend to be me while I check it out.' Because they were both wearing school uniforms, it was easy to do.

Kal frowned. 'What if you get caught?'

'It's worth the risk. I can't hack them if I don't know what software they're using. There's a storeroom marked on the map – over on the north side near the bathrooms Miss Biggs pointed out before the start of the race. I'll meet you there in ten minutes, okay?'

Kal was not sold on the idea but Dru didn't have the time to convince him. Kal took the glasses.

'Don't worry. No-one will see me.' Dru pointed to an air duct above their heads. 'You better catch-up with Regan before she blows a fuse.'

Kal smirked and ran off down the corridor.

Dru moved a few boxes and stacked them underneath the air duct, and carefully climbed up them until he could reach the roof. If the cover was nailed shut, his plan would be worthless, but luckily he pushed the grate easily, and pulled himself up into the ceiling.

He didn't exactly have great upper-body strength, but the adrenaline caused by the fear of getting caught certainly helped him out in this situation.

Once in the shaft, he carefully placed the grate back over the air duct and started crawling through the ceiling cavity. The hum of the air conditioning helped cover the creaking sounds he made as he slowly moved through the space. He looked at his watch. Only nine minutes to find *something* useful before he was out of time.

Dust from the vent tickled his nose and he sneezed loudly.

'Gesundheit.'

Dru's eyes widened and he froze.

'What did you say?' asked a female voice below the air vent.

'You know, just being polite,' answered a male voice.

'Whatever,' said the woman, sounding resigned. 'Now, pass me that test tube.'

Dru crawled faster, hoping no-one tried too hard to work out where the mystery sneeze had come from.

CHAPTER ELEVEN

In a pitch-black corridor, Regan was badgering her team.

'I can't see anything,' moaned an unhappy Chloe.

'Just keep feeling around,' ordered Regan.

'It's hopeless,' said a boy.

'Quit complaining, Lincoln. We just need to find the exit.'

The whole team was grumbling. Without a light source they were beginning to believe they might be stuck here, with Regan, the most unpleasant girl in school, for the rest of their lives.

Just at that moment Kal, wearing Dru's glasses, entered the corridor, shining his torch.

'Dru! Hooray!' a couple of the kids said. 'You're –'

But Regan didn't want Dru to be congratulated. She cut in. 'About time, Dru. We better not have lost because of you.'

Kal shone the torch on each of the walls, until the beam of light stopped to reveal a button near the ceiling. 'There!' shouted Kal.

Regan jumped up to hit it. A door opened and the team passed through with a collective sigh of relief.

On to the next challenge.

•

Dru, meanwhile, was concerned with his own private challenge: crawling through the air ducts without his glasses. He passed over a grate and could see two technicians below working on desktop computers, sharing information. One of them said, 'Sector Five F reporting GNOME interface is down.'

The second technician nodded. 'Great, running a diagnostic on the base Debian platform . . . I see the problem. Can you hand me that wedge? I need to access the source code to apply a patch.'

'Sure, I'll schedule a full service test of the APT frontend overnight.'

'Good idea,' the first technician replied, clearly pleased with the outcome.

Dru squinted, watching the second technician place his palm against a scanning device, which read his fingerprints. A drawer opened and he removed what Dru imagined was the wedge they'd been discussing: it resembled a crystal but had a silver connection like a USB.

Dru moved further along the air duct, and stopped over another grate. He could see into an empty room that looked like a prison hospital ward: beds, monitors, drips and medical equipment.

Dru had to stifle a gasp when he saw his aunt, Maya, enter the room with Dr Wenders. They were mid-argument. 'Listen carefully,' Dr Wenders said sternly. 'You need to look out for shaking, stiffening of the joints and a sudden spike in temperature.'

Maya nodded. 'I understand that viruses travel,' she replied with equal firmness. 'But it makes no sense that it would only impact one year group.'

'You're not here to question,' said Dr Wenders aggressively. 'You're here to observe. Nothing more.'

Even without his glasses Dru could see that his aunt was not going to be intimidated. 'I can't treat children if I don't know all the facts,' she said adamantly.

Dr Wenders held up his hand to silence his fellow doctor. 'The only *fact* you need to know is that several thousand Chinese students are now lying in an unresponsive state due to fever. And we don't want that to happen here.'

This time Dru could not contain his gasp. Fortunately, the doctors below didn't appear to hear him. He hurriedly moved further along the air duct, trying to process what he'd just heard.

•

Jiao and his team were huddled around another plinth; this one was positioned next to a stationary exercise bike, but thus far the team had no idea how the two were connected. Jiao had noticed that Kal was no longer with the group but didn't draw attention to it. Two of his teammates, Tamsin and Matt, were trying to solve a simultaneous maze using a gaming console to get to the centre at the same time. Their timing was wrong, and they kept having to start again. All the while a digital clock continued its countdown.

Matt was getting stressed. 'Why don't you get Kal to do this?' he asked.

Jiao was quick to cover for Kal's absence. 'Kal's completing another task for me.'

'Well, *you* do it, then.'

Jiao wasn't about to show his team he didn't have the enhanced skills they now had. 'We all need to do our part,' he said patiently. 'Breathe slowly. It's about precision, not speed.'

Matt sighed but responded well to Jiao's encouragement, and tried again. This time they both

completed the maze at the same time, to cheers from
their teammates.

A drawer opened in the plinth, and Jiao removed
a USB attached to a tag. He read the tag. 'You may
be fast, but can you last?' He looked up at his team.
'It must be an endurance test.'

Jiao handed the USB to Hannah, who inserted it
into the exercise bike and climbed on to the seat. She
began cycling at a furious pace until she reached a
certain speed and a light attached to the bike turned
on as a digital clock commenced a three-minute
countdown.

'You have to maintain that pace for three minutes,'
Jiao explained. 'You can do it!'

•

Dru's time was up. He'd taken a few wrong turns in
search of the storeroom where he was due to meet
Kal, all the while trying to hold his panic in check.
*'Several thousand Chinese students are now lying in an
unresponsive state due to fever.'* Dru kept repeating that

figure in his head as he crawled: *thousands*. What did it all mean? And were all his schoolmates now also at risk?

Finally he found the storeroom and prised the grate up, only to close it quickly again when he saw Regan enter below. Chloe joined her a moment later. They spoke in hushed tones. 'What time did they get home last night?' Regan asked.

Chloe hesitated before replying, 'Dru and Kal are my friends.'

Regan stepped forward, towering over Chloe. 'As Year Leader, I have the power to make things easier for you, Chloe. Or harder.'

Dru held his breath; it was all he could do.

But Chloe didn't seem to have it in her to stand up to Regan's bullying. She sighed. 'Kal got back just after seven. Dru and Jiao about half an hour later.'

Regan's delight in the girl's betrayal made Dru seethe from above. 'I *knew* they were up to something.' She gave Chloe an encouraging smile, clearly hoping to elicit more information from her.

Chloe fell for it. 'Don't you think it's weird that Jiao wouldn't take his necklace off for the game?'

But Regan didn't get the chance to answer, as Kal, still pretending to be Dru, opened the door to the storeroom, carrying the digital map. Kal was surprised to see the girls in there, but covered quickly. 'Hey, the map says we should go this way,' he said.

Annoyed at being interrupted, Regan gave him an angry glare. 'I know what the map says.' She grabbed the digital tablet and stormed out of the room with Chloe close behind her.

Kal looked up at the ceiling as Dru opened the grate overhead and dropped to the floor.

'Find anything out?' asked Kal as he handed over Dru's glasses.

Dru shook his head; where to even start? He put his glasses on. 'I'll tell you later.'

'Fine. There's no time now anyway. I have to get back to my team before they finish. We better win this scavenger hunt!'

The boys went their separate ways, each managing to rejoin their team without causing a fuss.

Kal caught up with Jiao's team at the completion of the course, in time to see Miss Biggs, watched by Dr Wenders and his aunt Maya, count the five found items in Jiao's bag. 'Well done, Jiao. Your team are the winners.'

Jiao looked proud and relieved. There were high-fives all round.

Regan came rushing into the room with her teammates, Dru with them.

Miss Biggs was less congratulatory. 'Not your best performance, Regan.'

'It was my team's fault, Miss,' Regan said.

This retort just seemed to disappoint Miss Biggs even more. 'A leader takes responsibility, Regan. You could learn from Jiao.'

Regan looked suddenly furious. 'No, Jiao's a liar! A fake! There's no way he beat us without cheating.' Regan lunged at Jiao and ripped off his necklace. 'And you shouldn't have been wearing this.'

Jiao tried to get the necklace back from her but it flew out of her hand, landing on the floor. Dr Wenders walked over and picked up the necklace, examining the glass vial closely, his eyes narrowing. He looked at Jiao with curiosity, then turned to one of the lab technicians hovering nearby. 'Take Jiao to the sick bay,' he said slowly and deliberately. 'He appears to be unwell.'

'No,' Jiao retorted, his panic showing. 'I feel fine! Please!' But the observers ushered Jiao out of the room.

Dru and Kal wanted to intervene and stop them from taking Jiao away but they couldn't afford to draw attention to themselves.

Maya stepped forward to go with them but Dr Wenders stopped her. 'You're not required, Dr Sharma.'

Dr Wenders moved over to show Miss Biggs the vial. 'Were you aware of this "necklace", Miss Biggs?'

Miss Biggs looked around, flustered, obviously upset by the turn of events and unsure how to answer.

Dr Wenders gave her a withering look. 'I think it's best you take these students back to school now.'

He turned and left the foyer, leaving Miss Biggs and her students alone in the entrance, feeling as though they had all just failed a major test.

Dru and Kal were devastated by the turn of events. What was going to happen to Jiao now?

CHAPTER TWELVE

The twins watched the school bus leave the Global Child Initiative headquarters on its way back to school. They had told Miss Biggs they'd get a lift home with their aunt.

They were not going to leave Jiao behind if they could help it, and they had a plan.

As they waited for Maya to appear in the carpark, Dru told Kal what he'd heard while travelling through the air ducts inside the building. 'Thousands of kids are seriously ill in China. I think it's the implant,' he blurted out to his brother.

Kal looked scared, his usual casual bravado gone. 'Is the same thing going to happen to us? I mean, to me?'

Dru shrugged, unsure, then nodded as he spotted Maya leaving the building and walking towards her car. Dru ducked out of sight and Kal ran over to the car.

Maya was surprised to see her nephew, 'Kal,' she said in surprise. 'What are you doing here?'

Kal pretended to be unwell. 'I told the teachers I'd get a lift with you because I'm not feeling –' Kal collapsed dramatically against the car.

'Kal!' Maya shouted, and Kal felt slightly guilty at her panic. 'You look terrible. Can you walk?'

Kal moaned.

Maya held on to Kal and ushered him back into the Global Child Initiative building. Once inside, she led him to a hospital bed, where he sat with his head in his hands as she got out her stethoscope to check his heartbeat. Kal glanced into the next room, where a curtain partially hid a boy lying down, inert, on a stretcher.

'Jiao? Jiao, wake up! What did they do to him?'

Maya looked around uncertainly, but before she could ask, Dr Wenders strode into the room. 'Dr Sharma? What are you doing here?'

Maya was caught off-guard. 'I brought in my nephew. He's feeling faint.'

Kal sprang to his feet 'Actually, I'm fine now. Must have been a stitch.'

His aunt looked at him. 'A stitch?'

'Dr Sharma,' Dr Wenders said sharply, 'you don't have authorisation to bring anyone into this area. You need to take that student out of here. Immediately.'

A different kind of concern spread over Maya's face; something more than mere worry over her nephew's health. She grabbed Kal's hand and led him from the room, both looking over their shoulders in confusion and fear.

•

Dru remained outside, tucked out of sight in the bushes, waiting for Kal and their aunt to reappear.

He was talking to Rose on the walkie-talkie, updating her on what had happened inside headquarters, but froze when a screech of tyres signalled a black van pulling into the carpark.

He crouched close to the ground and watched in horror as, a moment later, a stretcher was wheeled out of the building. There was no mistaking the boy lying unresponsive who was loaded unceremoniously into the van.

'Jiao!' Dru gasped.

On the other end of the walkie-talkie came a crackle, then Rose's voice calling out: 'Dru, what's happening? Is it Jiao? Is he there?'

Dru was transfixed, unable to respond as the van doors closed and his new friend was taken away.

Dru finally found his voice and clicked on the walkie-talkie. 'Jiao's been taken. I have to go.' He ended the conversation as he saw an angry-looking Maya march out of the building, pulling Kal by the arm in her wake.

'Kal! Bua!' Dru ran out from the bushes and into

the carpark, stopping only when he reached a grim-faced Maya.

'Both of you, get in the car,' she said. 'Now.'

Dru didn't understand what was happening, but he felt he had no choice. He got in with his brother.

'Where are they taking Jiao?' asked Dru as Maya drove out of the carpark. But Maya put a finger to her lips and turned the radio on, loud. They drove in a tense silence for a few minutes until they found a park close to home, where they got out of the car and watched the beautiful city lights.

Then Maya started talking. 'You need to tell me everything you know, boys. Were those kids in the tunnels running from the Global Child Initiative?'

The twins glanced at each other. It was a gamble but after what had happened with Jiao, they felt they needed to tell their aunt the truth. They nodded in unison.

'Why didn't you tell me?' she asked.

Both boys hesitated, then Kal finally spoke. 'We didn't know if we could trust you.'

Maya looked mortified. 'You know I would never hurt you, or any children, don't you?'

The boys looked sheepish. 'They're messing with kids' minds. They could have done the same to you,' explained Dru.

Maya looked slowly from Dru to Kal, then back, clearly stunned. 'Mind control?'

Dru nodded. 'Our year group was implanted with some sort of device during the free dental check-up.'

'And it happened at Jiao's school too,' Kal added.

'There's been an outbreak of fever among the students in China,' said Maya, her words almost tripping over themselves. 'They're worried about the same thing happening here.'

'The implant they're using is some kind of microprocessor that enhances athletic and academic ability.'

Maya looked incredulous, until Kal picked up a huge, heavy rock and threw it a fair distance away.

'But that's impossible!' Maya said, then she looked to Dru. 'Can you do that too?'

Dru shook his head before he went on to explain about the dental check. That Kal had been implanted twice and Dru had no enhanced anything.

Finally Maya stopped him. 'That's enough. This is too much. How have you boys been dealing with this on your own? Let's get back in the car. We're telling your parents, and then we're going to the authorities.'

But both boys refused to move. 'We can't, Bua. The authorities didn't help Tim. His memory was wiped and his parents are missing,' said Dru.

'We can't let anything happen to Mum or Dad,' finished Kal.

Maya slowly shook her head, unsure of what to do next. Everything she believed to be true about the Global Child Initiative and its interest in helping the world's children had just gone up in flames. And even worse, it was clear her family, the people she loved most in the world, were in grave danger.

CHAPTER THIRTEEN

Back in the tunnels, the Unlisted were feeling low. They weren't sure what had happened with Jiao but they knew it was bad. They had put their own lives in danger to help another unlisted teenager, and it had been a waste of time – they couldn't save him. Would whatever was happening to him eventually happen to them?

Rose was lying down, trying to sleep, but her thoughts were racing and her eyes remained open.

Suddenly Gemma stood up and moved to grab her belongings, shoving them into a bag.

'Gemma, what are you doing?'

'You heard what happened to Jiao,' spat out Gemma. 'I'm not sitting around waiting for them to take me away too.'

'They're not going to take you, Gem. No-one knows we're here,' pointed out Jacob gently.

Kymara took a more direct approach. 'Do you think you'll be safer out there?'

'Don't make any rash decisions,' Rose urged. 'It's been a tough day, for all of us. We need sleep. Things might look better in the morning.'

Gemma slumped to the ground, defeated and exhausted.

•

Bright and early the next morning Dadi swept into the lounge room carrying a drink, and saw her daughter sleeping on the couch. 'This proves it,' she said beaming, waking Maya with a kiss. 'None of my children can bear to be away from me.'

Maya, wrapped in a pashmina shawl and still in

her clothes from the previous night, sat up wearily. 'Hi, Mum.'

Dadi ruffled her daughter's hair. 'Anyone sleeping on the couch instead of in their own bed is bound to wake up feeling shabby, no? Nothing my special lassi can't fix.' She handed Maya the drink and Maya took a grateful sip.

Dru and Kal appeared in the lounge room, both still in their pyjamas.

Dadi frowned. 'All three of you look very tired. What did you get up to last night?'

Dru answered: 'Video games.'

Maya answered: 'Bowling.'

Kal answered: 'An escape room.'

All at the same time.

Dadi looked confused, and they tried again.

Dru said: 'Bowling.'

Kal said: 'Video games.'

And Maya tried: 'Escape room.'

Dadi waited a moment, and then gave a wry smile. 'No wonder you're all so tired. Too many activities in one night! You need a good breakfast.'

She left the room and Maya turned to the boys. 'We have to get our story straight!' The boys nodded in agreement.

Maya continued. 'And I'm resigning from the Global Child Initiative this morning.'

'No!' said Dru immediately. 'You can't. They'll know something's up.'

Kal backed up his brother. 'We need you to help us find out what's going on.'

Maya shook her head. 'I don't want to be a part of whatever horrid experiment is taking place in that building.'

'You can help us stop whatever's going on, Bua. They just took Jiao away and no-one stopped them,' said Dru, plaintively.

•

The Sharma family were at the breakfast table and halfway through a plate of parathas before Dadi noticed Jiao's absence.

'Oh. But where is Jiao? I'll go get him,' Dadi said, moving towards the staircase.

The boys looked at each other. 'Um, Jiao isn't here,' said Dru quickly. 'He . . . he's still at school, part of a science experiment into sleep patterns . . .'

Dadi did not look impressed. 'Really? The school should have let us know.'

Maya helped out. 'I – er . . . gave him permission.'

Dadi did not look any more impressed. 'Well, that is a big shame because I put green algae in the parathas just for him.'

The Sharma family stopped chewing as one. *Green algae?!*

•

'Gemma?'

Jacob stopped mid-stretch, his sleepiness vanishing as panic set in. Looking around he saw Kymara and Rose sleeping. But Gemma was nowhere in sight. He scrambled to pull on his shoes, and slipped out of the room, making his way down the tunnel, on full alert. Still no sign of Gemma.

He came out into the morning sun, blinking so his eyes could adjust. He kept to the shadows of the trees as he moved through the park. Then he saw her.

On the far side of a hill, tucked away from view, Gemma lay outstretched, her face turned towards the sun, her eyes closed.

Jacob moved closer. 'Cool spot,' he said with a smile.

Gemma's eyes flashed open, hyper alert.

'Don't worry. It's just me,' reassured Jacob.

'You gave me a heart attack,' she said.

Jacob lay on the grass next to Gemma, soaking in the morning rays. 'How good is that sun?'

'How did you find me?' Gemma said, half-pouting and half-smiling at the intrusion.

Jacob laughed. 'Really, farm girl? I just looked for the grass and the trees.'

Gemma smiled.

'Out here you can kid yourself you're back home,' said Jacob.

She nodded. 'Yeah, the treehouse I'd grown out of but still liked to climb into . . . sometimes . . . just over there.'

Jacob nodded. 'And at my house, just over there, a full fridge and a cupboard full of snacks. And our dogs. And fighting over control of the TV remote . . .'

It felt good to spend just a few seconds remembering out loud how normal their lives had been.

•

Dadi pushed open the twins' bedroom door as they were gathering their school work. 'Boys, you have a visitor,' said Dadi. 'I'm sure they'll help in any way they can,' she said before disappearing again.

'Thank you, Mrs Sharma.' A middle-aged man with blond hair and a Scottish accent stepped into the room and partially closed the door.

Dru and Kal had never seen this man before in their lives, but he smiled like a crocodile, cold and measured. They instantly knew he wasn't to be trusted.

The man looked at each twin in turn. 'Nice to meet you, boys,' he said. 'I'm Mr Cunningham, and we will be seeing a lot more of each other at Westbrook High. But for now I'm here to collect Jiao's things. His grandfather is very ill in China, and he had to return home unexpectedly.'

Before Kal could even exchange a look with his brother, Dru spoke confidently, almost nonchalantly. 'We'll gather his stuff together for you,' he said. 'We can bring it to you downstairs.'

But Mr Cunningham didn't take the hint. He stayed put. 'Did Jiao say anything unusual to you?'

The boys feigned confusion. 'About what?'

Mr Cunningham leant in. 'Did he ever mention implants?'

The boys looked at each other briefly and then shook their heads. 'No,' they replied in unison.

Cunningham watched them both for a moment, then, seemingly satisfied, tapped a password into the digital tablet he carried. Kal's head dropped to his chest instantly. He remained motionless. Dru quickly followed his example, slumping, terrified he was going to get caught out.

He watched from the corner of his eye as Mr Cunningham rifled through books and other papers on Kal's desk. He zipped up Jiao's half-full suitcase and then stopped as he looked in the direction of the laptop sticking out of Dru's school bag.

Dru forced himself to remain rigid as Mr Cunningham opened the computer, only to find the screen locked. He tried a couple of passwords but couldn't get in. Dru could sense the man's building frustration and almost laughed when he heard Dadi call from downstairs, 'I've made some chai, Stephen!'

Mr Cunningham shoved Dru's laptop back in the school bag and called out, 'Thank you, but I can't stay.' He grabbed Jiao's suitcase, tapped a password into his digital tablet and left the room.

Kal's head lifted as though nothing had happened. Dru stared at him. 'We've just been raided.'

Kal looked perplexed. 'What are you talking about?'

CHAPTER FOURTEEN

'What's the last thing you remember from this morning?' Dru asked his brother as they walked their bikes into the school grounds.

Kal searched his memory. 'Algae parathas,' he said.

'And nothing after that?' prompted Dru. 'Nothing upstairs later, in our room?'

Kal shook his head.

Dru said aloud what he was thinking. 'He wiped your memory.'

The boys locked up their bikes and walked to class.

'Who wiped my memory?' said Kal, failing to keep the fear out of his voice.

But they were joined by their classmates and the conversation was cut short.

A moment after the boys took their seats in class Mr Cunningham entered the room. Dru looked at Kal to check whether his twin recognised the teacher as the man who had been in their home only an hour earlier. Kal shook his head minimally at Dru.

'Welcome to your new classroom. My name is Mr Cunningham.'

'Good morning, Mr Cunningham,' the class parroted back.

'I'll be your class teacher from now on.'

Chloe put up her hand. 'Where's Mr Park?'

'Gone,' said Mr Cunningham abruptly. 'But I have some exciting news,' he went on. 'This class has been chosen to participate in the Global Child Congress. This will be an opportunity to showcase the progress you've made under the Global Child Initiative. From now on, you'll be divided into three colour-coded groups.'

Mr Cunningham brought up a simple presentation on the smart board. There were three words: BASIC, CORE and ELITE. 'You will remain in these groups for all activities moving forward,' he continued as the students murmured in surprise. 'And each group will have special responsibilities on the day of the Congress.'

Mr Cunningham pointed out an open box on his desk. Inside the box were red, green and yellow ties – red was for Elite, green was for Core and yellow was for Basic – along with matching wristbands.

'As I call out your name, come and collect your kit,' he said.

He consulted his tablet. 'Elite group: Tim Hale, Regan Holcroft, Drupad Sharma, Kalpen Sharma.'

Tim moved up to the desk and took his red tie.

'Core group . . .' Mr Cunningham continued calling out the names of everyone in the class.

●

Rose and Kymara were sorting through the remainder of their supplies when a sound echoed through the tunnels.

They jumped up, but before they could hide, Jacob and Gemma arrived at the hide-out.

Rose was instantly on them. 'Where have you been?'

'Just grabbing some fresh air,' said Jacob. He looked at Rose meaningfully. 'We're all good.'

Rose walked over to Gemma, softening her approach. 'Gemma, the only way we're going to survive is to stick together.'

Gemma did not look convinced. 'And do what, exactly?'

'Why don't we start with this?' offered up Kymara. She held the list Dru had printed out for her. 'These kids responded to my post.'

'I don't want to risk our safety to find them,' said Rose.

'We can't just abandon them,' said Kymara.

Jacob backed up Kymara. 'You've said it before, Rose – we need all the friends we can get.' But then he frowned. 'Although how do we find them when we have no internet access?'

Everyone fell silent, thinking. Then Gemma brightened. 'We go old school,' she said with a grin.

•

At Westbrook High, Dru and Kal – now wearing the red ties of the Elite group – were walking to their lockers, speaking in hushed tones.

'If they're deleting my memories, what else are they doing to my head?' asked Kal, freaked out by this new development.

'I don't know,' answered Dru, 'but I bet they're doing worse to Jiao. We need to find out what happened to him.'

Kal nodded. 'Miss Biggs has files on all of us in her office. Maybe we can sneak in and have a look.'

Without another word they veered off down the corridor and headed in the direction of Miss Biggs' office, passing Chloe walking with Regan. Chloe looked at Dru and said hi, but he refused to answer or look her in the eye.

'We can't trust Chloe,' said Dru to Kal. It hurt him to admit it, but she was no longer the girl next door that he'd not-so-secretly had a crush on for years.

They arrived outside Miss Biggs' office to find the door not completely shut. Dru and Kal checked that the coast was clear before pushing the door open and slipping inside.

What they weren't expecting to see was Mr Cunningham bent over, searching through Miss Biggs filing cabinets. He sat back up, and gave a fake smile.

'Can I help you, boys?'

Caught off-guard, Kal stuttered, 'Uh . . . we're looking for Miss Biggs.'

Mr Cunningham looked intently at the twins. 'Miss Biggs is no longer with the Initiative. Or at this school. Is there anything I can do for you?'

'No, thanks. See you later!' Dru replied, and he and Kal retreated quickly out of the office and headed out into the playground.

They stood together, as kids manoeuvred around them. To an outsider, everything would have looked normal: boys and girls kicking balls, gossiping, eating lunch, but all the while Dru and Kal were trying to come to terms with everything that had happened in the past twenty-four hours.

'First they make Mr Park disappear, and now Miss Biggs is gone too?' said Dru. 'I thought she was one of them.'

Kal nodded. 'And that new guy, Mr Cunningham. What if he has more control over my brain than I do?'

The school bell sounded and all of a sudden the chaos of the playground disappeared and was replaced by students falling into neat lines, their glazed expressions showing Dru that once again they were under the control of the Global Child Initiative.

The Elite leaders, wearing their red ties, moved to the front of the groups. Dru scrambled to do the same.

Regan called out to the students in a monotone. 'Each of you is to obey your designated leader without question. Begin endurance drills!'

Behind her, Mr Cunningham kept a watchful eye on proceedings, often checking his tablet. For the next twenty minutes the group went through a range of exercises, from jogging on the stop to push-ups to star jumps. It was an extreme synchronised workout. The Elites at the front – including Kal – did nothing, merely standing still, so Dru copied everything Kal did.

Eventually, the exercises stopped and the kids broke back into normal behaviour, wondering why they were so sweaty, but otherwise going about their business as though nothing unusual had occurred.

Kal, however, knew something had happened, but he didn't know exactly what. He looked at his brother, fear etched in his face. 'How long was I out? What did they make me do this time?'

CHAPTER FIFTEEN

Wearing hats that covered their faces, Gemma and Kymara crept down a back alleyway in a quiet suburb. A car slowed as it passed, making the girls stop and turn their faces away instinctively, hearts pounding. The car moved on.

The girls made their way down another laneway until Gemma gestured for Kymara to stop in front of a closed gate. She ran her hands along the top of the fence line, then paused and grinned as she held up a hidden key. She carefully inserted it in the lock, and the gate clicked open, allowing Gemma and Kymara to walk up the path to the house.

It was an old single storey brick house that had seen better days. The garden was overgrown and the house needed a paint job, but to the girls, who had lived in a filthy tunnel for the past few days, it looked like heaven.

At the front door Gemma knocked and waited, but there was no answer. She led Kymara around the side of the house and the girls carefully climbed in through an unlocked window. The room was gloomily dark, and lined with dusty old bookshelves. But instead of books, the shelves were heaped with bits of old lo-fi tech. Reel-to-reel tape machines, VHS players, old film cameras. Piles and piles of tangled leads and old screens.

Gemma knew exactly what she was looking for in this house, and quickly moved over to two ham radios, one smaller than the other, set up in a corner. They were old fashioned, rectangular pieces of equipment with a range of dials and knobs. She turned on the larger radio.

'So, this is how we fly under the radar – ham radio,'

said Gemma, looking happier than she had in days. 'It gives us access to frequency allocations right through the RF spectrum.'

Kymara looked at her blankly. 'Now in English, please,' she said, but her friend's enthusiasm was infectious.

Gemma continued. 'With this we can communicate locally, across the country, or even with astronauts on the space station. Cool, huh?' She picked up the receiver. 'This is Farm Girl Three Hundred. Farm Girl Three Hundred. Does anyone read me?'

Suddenly, out of the darkness a fierce voice boomed: 'What do you think you're doing?'

Gemma and Kymara froze as an old woman wearing a long woollen cardigan and unkempt curly grey hair hobbled towards them. She laughed. 'Your voice hasn't changed, Gemma. How are your parents?'

Gemma turned, nervous. 'Hello, Mae.'

The woman came a little closer, and Kymara could tell she was blind. Her eyes were covered in a filmy glow and she wasn't quite looking at them as she spoke.

'You used to be a good kid, Gemma. But here you are, breaking in like a common thief. Messing with my radio. My only link with the outside world. Who's your friend?'

'Hi, I'm Kymara. Please don't call the cops.'

Gemma sighed. 'We're in trouble, Mae. It's a long story.'

'Wouldn't dream of calling the cops, love.'

Gemma smiled. 'Mum and Dad always said that you were a bit of a . . . an outsider.'

Mae threw her head back and laughed. 'An "outsider"? Got to love a euphemism. I was queer before we even had a word for it. The weird, queer, blind kid. I know what it means to be an outlaw. Don't you worry, girls,' she added with a grin, 'I'm on your side, whatever you've done.'

•

'Argh, this maths sucks!' Kal moaned as he and Dru sat at the kitchen table doing their homework. He couldn't concentrate; his frustration and anger were mixing with the fear that he could no longer control the thoughts in his brain.

Dru, next to him, was working through his homework with no problems, helping himself to snacks.

Kal was getting angrier and angrier. It wasn't fair. And what would happen next? What would he be forced to do without his knowledge? He stood up suddenly, flinging the chair behind him onto the floor.

'I want my life back! I want my brain back!' he said as he ran out of the room.

•

The more modern-looking ham radio Mae had brought out helped Gemma as she searched through Kymara's list of possible unlisted teens.

Mae had not asked any further questions and left them alone to get on with their task.

They had tried to contact the first three, with no answer. Gemma moved on to the fourth name.

'This is Farm Girl Three Hundred. Do you read me, Mack Attack One?' said Gemma into the receiver.

Kymara was impatient. 'Move on, Gemma, he's not responding. Try a different one.' But Gemma's determination paid off as a crackle sounded over the air waves and a boy's voice said, 'You're not the only Steve in Zomville.' The girls looked at each other and high-fived. A response!

'Farm Girl Three Hundred, reading you loud and clear, Mack Attack One.'

For a moment there was silence, and then an emotional Mack responded over the airwaves: 'I'm scared. Please help me.'

Gemma and Kymara's earlier excitement died down immediately as the weight of the connection hit them. This was a boy who desperately needed them – but how were they going to help him when they couldn't even help themselves?

•

Dru ran up the stairs after Kal and found him already in the bedroom, holding a pair of pliers. He looked wide-eyed and furious.

'Whoa. What are you doing with those?' asked Dru.

'I'm ripping this thing out of my head right now, before they do anything else to me!' said Kal, as he opened his mouth and positioned the pliers over a tooth.

Dru leapt forward. 'Kal! Stop!'

Kal wrestled Dru off easily – Dru was no match for his brother's newfound strength – and was about to try again when Maya appeared in their doorway.

Kal turned to his aunt. 'Please hold Dru back while I pull this implant out of my teeth,' he said desperately.

But Maya snatched the pliers away from Kal. 'There's no way to remove an implant, Kal. It's embedded in the jawbone.'

'But . . . Jiao?' asked Dru in confusion.

'Jiao's device must have been implanted incorrectly. I've been digging around, seen reports, scans. Once these things are in, they can't be removed.'

The finality of this hit Kal, and he dropped onto his bed, staring straight ahead.

'What else were you able to find out today? Do

you know where they've taken Jiao?' Dru asked hopefully.

Maya looked from Dru to Kal, and then back again. 'I wish I had good news, but . . . Jiao has been sent back to China.'

'Did they implant him? Is he going to get the same fever as the other kids there?' asked Kal.

Maya shook her head sadly. 'I'm sorry, I don't know. But I found out something else,' she said, showing the boys her phone. On it was a list of names.

Dru read out the names he recognised: 'Kymara, Jacob, Gemma, Rose . . .' He looked at Maya, alarmed.

'Infinity Group has a list of every kid who hasn't been implanted . . . except for you, Dru,' she said.

The boys looked shocked.

And Maya's bad news wasn't over yet. 'And they're about to launch a massive search for all of them,' she said.

CHAPTER **SIXTEEN**

Dru walks through the tunnel at night. It is dripping wet and dark. Shadows loom large. The torch he has brought with him keeps flickering out. 'Hello, can anyone hear me?'

There is no answer but the moan of the wind as it blows through the tunnels. Faces of people he knows — Regan, his brother — flash in front of him but disappear as he comes closer. Dru has never been so scared in his life. Where have his friends gone? Where is his brother? How is he ever going to get out of this tunnel alive? A creepy voice suddenly yells into his ear: 'There's no escape. Wake up!'

Dru woke with a start, confused, sweating. His heart was racing. He heard a deep groan and looked over to see Dadi dragging Kal out of bed by his ankles.

'Dadi! What time is it?' moaned Kal. 'Please, let me sleep.'

Dadi was not taking no for an answer this morning. 'Time to wake up, my lazy wombats! *Up, up, up.* Your wonderful bua is on the breakfast news. That makes me famous by association! *Move it.*'

She swept out of the room and back downstairs. By the time the boys dragged themselves into the kitchen Dadi was seated at the end of the table, watching the news report. An immaculately dressed businesswoman, Emma Ainsworth, was holding a press conference on the steps of Parliament House. Maya was by her side as she made her announcement. Anousha, Rahul and Vidya gathered behind Dadi to watch the report, eating breakfast as they watched.

'Thank you for coming today. I'm known in the tech world as an innovator and a disruptor, but I'm also a great believer in giving children a brighter future,' said Emma, speaking to the camera. 'That's why I'm Chair of the Global Child Initiative, a pilot program that has been rolled out to every school in the country.'

Rahul was impressed. 'You're doing that,' he said to his boys. 'Didn't have any initiatives like that when I was at school.'

The boys remained glued to the screen. A reporter was asking, 'Ms Ainsworth, you're launching a privately funded Child Location Program. Does this reflect a failure on the part of the government?'

Emma considered her response and answered diplomatically: 'I would never be so bold as to suggest that. But I am proud to announce, as of today, the Global Child Initiative will be putting real boots on the ground in the hope of locating homeless and vulnerable children. We plan to keep looking all across Australia. We believe that every child deserves the academic and medical advantages that come with participation in our program.'

Dadi was nodding at the screen, buying into every word Emma Ainsworth was saying.

Dru and Kal looked at each other. So, this is what Maya had told them last night. It was the beginning. The start of the hunt for the unlisted kids all around the country, cloaked as a social good.

When Maya was no longer on the screen, Dadi turned the television off and started clearing the table. 'Okay, that's enough excitement for one day, my little wombats. You will be late. Get a wriggle on!'

•

A trio of drones descended towards the rail lines. One drone buzzed ominously along a nearby street as a Global Child Initiative van headed in the other direction. Four uniformed guards walked through the alleys of the city.

Jacob was on his way out of the tunnels to source breakfast for the Unlisted when he spotted two suited guards stop a group of teenagers on the stairs leading down from the Harbour Bridge. He crouched behind the wrought-iron gate, staying hidden while keeping the scene in view.

During the course of the conversation Jacob saw one of the guards check the teens' status on an electronic tablet. He nodded to his co-worker and the teens were allowed to pass.

One of the guards glanced in Jacob's direction, and he melted back into the darkness, hoping he hadn't been seen. He stayed deathly still and silent for a few moments before daring to peek out again – but all he saw was the two guards continuing down the steps and away.

Jacob steadied his breathing and looked around him again; could he risk leaving the tunnel entrance? Then he saw it: a low-flying drone hovering nearby. That was it; there was no way he was heading out there with this much visible surveillance. The Unlisted would have to go without breakfast this morning . . . but then his stomach rumbled. And he had to reconsider.

•

Dru and Kal both felt unnerved the moment they entered the quadrangle at Westbrook High School to see students sweeping and cleaning up rubbish. They all wore their yellow ties, the Basic colour, and they didn't look happy to be cleaning the yard before school.

Before either twin could comment on the changed conditions, Mr Cunningham's voice bellowed from a nearby corridor. 'Kalpen! Drupad! Tardiness is not appropriate for Elites. Please join Regan and Tim in the Elite common room, *immediately.*'

The boys looked at each other. 'What's he talking about?' hissed Dru. 'We don't have an Elite common room.'

Mr Cunningham signalled for the boys to follow him, which they did, curious, as he led them into a room that had been converted into a casual area strewn with beanbags, a comfy-looking couch and a foosball table.

Regan and Tim were already seated at a large round table, and the twins joined them.

'You should all be very proud of yourselves,' said Mr Cunningham, remaining standing so he towered over the students. 'Reaching this level of leadership within the Global Child Initiative is something to be celebrated.'

'Sir,' said Kal, 'is this room just for us?'

Mr Cunningham nodded. 'Being an Elite comes with rewards, but not without responsibilities.' He handed each of them a shiny black folder with a GLOBAL CHILD INITIATIVE logo emblazoned on it.

Kal flicked his folder open. 'Coooooool. One free period every day.'

'New school lunches based on the dietary needs of each Elite student,' read out Regan, impressed.

Tim read out the lines: 'Private training with premier sport and fitness coaches.'

Kal's concerns seemed to have vanished in light of the proffered rewards. 'Yes! Full complimentary access to the Adrenoblast Action Zone!'

Dru was showing less enthusiasm than the others, and Mr Cunningham was watching him carefully. 'I understand you are a keen student, Dru. This will interest you.' He pointed to a particular paragraph in the folder.

Dru read aloud: 'Highgate – a six-month residential experience. A unique program that nurtures students' rapid social, physical and mental growth.'

Mr Cunningham grinned at Dru. 'An opportunity next year if you stay on task. Six months parent-free – sounds cool, doesn't it?'

Mr Cunningham turned his attention back to the group. 'Remember, you must be our eyes and ears in the playground – make sure others are observing the rules and keeping the Global Child Initiative standards. Your position as Elites depends on it.'

Kal, Regan and Tim were nodding enthusiastically. Dru tried to join in but the whole thing was making him feel sick.

'Now, off to class.' Mr Cunningham left, followed by Kal and Regan.

Dru looked desperately at Tim, hoping he could get through. 'Tim? Doesn't this seem nuts to you?'

Tim looked at Dru blankly.

'Tim, have your parents come home yet?' asked Dru.

Tim looked confused. 'Come home from where? They didn't go anywhere.'

Dru had no idea how to counter that. Instead he read from his folder: 'Cores and Basics may not socialise with Elites without permission. The lowest-performing Cores will join Basics in cleaning duties.'

'We're Elites, Dru,' said Tim blithely. 'Don't worry about them.' He grabbed his bag and headed off to class. Dru was left alone in the Elite common room, feeling isolated and deeply concerned.

CHAPTER SEVENTEEN

Gemma's frustration was growing. 'She said she'd be on three-zero-zero-eight!'

Kymara scoffed as Gemma pressed buttons and glared at the ham radio as if willing it to work. 'Give her a break. Mae's ancient; she's, like, a hundred – maybe she got her numbers confused. And it's not like the reception in these tunnels is anything to brag about.'

A crackle rang out of the radio. There was no mistaking Mae's voice. 'Ancient? *Really?*'

'Mae! We thought maybe we were doing it wrong,'

said Gemma, desperately pleased to hear her old friend's voice.

'It sounds like you're doing fine,' Mae replied. 'Your friend called through last night. He's out near Wangaratta, said he'd be on one-two-three-three-two. Good luck, you rebels! Over and out.'

Gemma dialled the numbers, fine-tuning the frequency until a voice could be heard. 'Hello, hello? Anyone there?'

'We're here,' said Gemma, relieved. 'Is that Mack Attack One?'

Rose grabbed the receiver. 'Where are you?'

There was a pause but then Mack responded. 'A truck stop, I think a few hours out of Sydney. I've been stowing away in trucks, I didn't know what else to do.'

Gemma looked at Rose. They may have been living in a dingy tunnel, but at least they had a home and they were together. 'Can you get to Sydney?' she asked Mack.

'I think so. If I can find a truck heading that way.'

'We'll help you. I promise. You just have to get here,' said Gemma.

Rose gave Gemma an exasperated look and grabbed the receiver, covering the speaker with one hand. 'Gemma! We can't promise that.'

Gemma stood her ground. 'He's all alone, Rose. We can't leave him.' She grabbed the receiver back and spoke to Mack. 'Don't worry! We'll find you.'

She could feel Mack's relief through the radio. There was a pause before he asked one more question. 'Who are you guys?'

The three girls look at each other, for a brief moment relishing their status.

'We're The Unlisted,' Gemma said proudly. 'And so are you.'

•

The other Unlisted – Dru – was standing in line with his fellow students at Westbrook High to try the new lunch menu. Dru watched Kal grab a tray piled with delicious-looking food including a burger and fresh berries. He was clearly thrilled. 'I could get used to this,' he crowed as he moved over to a table.

Next in line was Chloe. In contrast to Kal's fare she was handed a tray with a messed-up-looking ham sandwich on it. It was as though someone had stepped on it on purpose before serving it up. 'This is insane,' she said, outraged. 'Why should they get better meals than us?'

She looked around at her peers, hoping for support, but no-one acknowledged her outburst. A smug-looking Regan and Tim collected their meals and headed to the leaders' table where Kal was already seated.

Dru stepped up to collect his tray as another boy in their class – a Core – complained about the quality of his meal. Mr Cunningham marched over to the boy and gave him a stern talking-to.

Dru grabbed his tray and sat next to his brother. Kal seemed different somehow. He seemed to be enjoying the hierarchy. Ever since he'd found out about the common room he'd become more arrogant, like he deserved everything he was being given. And Dru couldn't tell if it was the implant or his brother that was driving this change.

Chloe stood looking around at the tables – the Basics in one section; the Cores in another – then marched over to Dru and Kal's table and defiantly sat down.

Kal shook his head. 'Better not, Chloe. You read the rules about Basics and Elites mixing. Your area is over there.'

Chloe was indignant. 'Really?' Kal refused to look at her. She turned to Dru. 'Please, guys . . . don't do this.' None of the Elites responded. Dru looked deeply uncomfortable but he said nothing. 'These rules are stupid,' she pushed on. 'I can't believe you'd go along with them. We're *friends*.'

Regan was unmoved by her emotional performance. She looked Chloe squarely in the eye. 'It's this simple,' she said. 'You're Basic. Kal, make her go away. She's your responsibility.'

Mr Cunningham stood a short distance away, observing the situation. Kal stood up. Under his breath Dru begged him to sit down, but his brother wouldn't listen.

'I'm sorry, Chloe. You're forcing me to do this.' He grabbed a nearby rubbish bin and gave it to Chloe. 'Clean the quad, *Basic*.'

'Dru, can't you stop him?' Chloe said. Dru felt her eyes on him. He looked up and caught Mr Cunningham glaring at him. Once again he averted his eyes, feeling helpless and embarrassed. Chloe looked around to all the students, seeking support from the other Basics, anyone. 'You can't treat me like this,' she cried. 'I'm going to tell my parents!'

Silence fell in the lunch room as all the other Basics and Cores stared down at their plates, not wanting to get into trouble.

Mr Cunningham stepped forward and said with a smirk. 'If you want to tell your parents that you're failing the world's most advanced education program, go ahead. I should warn you that you'll be forfeiting your chance to advance to a Core, or maybe even an Elite.'

Chloe's shoulders slumped. Giving in to the humiliation, she picked up the bin and began to collect rubbish.

Mr Cunningham patted Kal on the back. 'Excellent work, Kalpen. A great example of leadership.'

Dru sat frozen, his appetite lost, watching Regan, Tim and Kal delightedly tuck into their burgers as if nothing had happened.

•

Jacob limped back along the dark tunnel, towards the hide-out. He had found the courage to head out to collect food for the group, but it had scared him.

Kymara and Rose ran to meet him, excited by the haul. A hungry Rose asked, 'How did you go?' Both girls went to grab the stash but the look on Jacob's face made them stop.

'Jacob? What's wrong?' asked Rose.

'Something's changed out there. There are Global Child Officers everywhere. They're stopping kids, scanning people.'

'We've seen this before,' said Rose.

Jacob shook his head. 'Not like this. There are drones.'

'Drones?' Kymara repeated, processing the information.

'They seemed to be searching for something.' He looked behind him, spooked. 'Let's get further inside.'

When the three arrived at the hide-out, Gemma was talking into the radio receiver. 'Okay, over and out.' She turned to the others. 'He's closer than he thought. It won't be long before he reaches Sydney.'

Gemma held out a couple of torn pages from an old Sydways city map, pointing to where he thought he was. 'He overheard the driver saying that they were going to stop here to eat in an hour.'

'An hour? We can't meet him in daylight! We'll have to wait until it's dark.'

'If we leave him out there by himself, he'll get caught for sure,' said Jacob.

Rose pondered this for a moment. 'Fine, but Gemms and I will go. It's not worth putting us all at risk.'

Shortly after, the two girls were ready to leave. Kymara brought the four of them in for a group hug. 'Be careful, all right?' she said to them.

Rose nodded seriously and then left with Gemma.

'What now?' asked Kymara when she and Jacob were left alone.

Jacob looked around. 'Guess we're not leaving here anytime soon.'

CHAPTER EIGHTEEN

At Westbrook High the kids were seated at their desks, talking, slowly getting their books out for class when Mr Cunningham entered the room. 'All right, students. We're going to take a break from our usual maths class to talk about something important.'

The students quietened down.

'As you know, there are unfortunate children out there who don't have the opportunities you take for granted.'

The smartboard lit up behind him and young faces began to appear, the faces of 'missing children'. Dru watched as familiar faces flicked up alongside many others. He was trying to stay calm, to not look scared, but seeing his new friends' photos on the board in front of him was freaking him out.

Mr Cunningham continued. 'We've sent these images to each and every one of you. You can access them on the school app. If you come across any of these children, don't approach them, help us to help them by informing us immediately. You are all, in your own way, essential to the success of the Global Child Initiative.'

After class Kal walked through the school grounds listening to an upbeat, thumping hip-hop track. Dru walked behind him, frustrated. He hated to see his brother look as though he didn't care about what was happening all around him. He grabbed the headphones from Kal's head, making Kal spin around, angry.

'We gotta talk,' said Dru.

Kal grabbed the headphones back from Dru and kept walking.

'Kal! We have to warn the Unlisted about what's happening.'

Kal sighed. 'Why?'

'Because they're our friends,' said Dru. 'And now half the city's out looking for them.'

'They'll be fine. They've kept themselves hidden for this long.'

'*What* is going on with you today?' Dru asked his brother.

'Nothing's wrong with me. I feel great. Chill, bro.'

But Dru hadn't finished. 'The way you treated Chloe . . . now the Unlisted . . . it's like the Global Child Initiative's using that thing in your head to turn off your feelings.'

Kal spun around and shoved his brother. 'Listen, Dru, it's time we looked after *us*. I'm not gonna feel guilty because I'm Elite and Chloe isn't, or some kids we hardly know are living in tunnels. That's their business.' He put his headphones back in, and – music thumping – continued on his way to the bike racks.

Dru stopped, and watched his brother walk away. He wasn't even sure he recognised him anymore.

•

Rose and Gemma were on high alert as they walked down the street on the way to their rendezvous point with Mack. Rose motioned to Gemma and they crossed the road, darting down a laneway. They emerged beside a set of steps leading down to another street below, and Rose signalled to Gemma to follow. Gemma consulted the crumpled map in her hands and nodded. They travelled on, running down stairs. Moments later a van passed by driven by a Global Child Initiative security guard.

•

Jacob and Kymara were fossicking through piles of debris and abandoned bric-a-brac, searching for anything that might brighten up their space. 'If we're gonna have a visitor,' Kymara had reasoned, giving Jacob a light punch on the arm to which he gave a slow smile, 'maybe we should give this place a makeover.'

Kymara kicked a bundle of papers and the stack toppled over, revealing a music magazine. She flicked it open to an old picture of a girl band from the early twenty-tens. She laughed. 'Something for your bedroom wall, Jacob?'

'I think I'll go for something a bit classier,' he replied as he headed back out to a recycling dump he'd seen earlier.

Kymara was hesitant. 'But you said there were drones out there.'

'They'll have moved on by now,' Jacob replied. 'I'll come back if I see anything. Promise,' he said, and he left her alone in the tunnels, leaving the grate open.

A short while later Kymara was reading some of the really out-of-date magazines when she heard a strange, sudden hum. Her eyes widened in panic and she stood up and flattened herself against the wall, hiding in the shadows.

At the entrance of the tunnels a drone dropped down, appearing in the light at the mouth of the drain. The drone's red sensor flickered and a strong beam of light shone into the tunnel, illuminating the darkness. It hummed and entered, slowly moving down the main tunnel.

Kymara kept flattened against the wall. She heard the noise and saw the light from the drone coming closer. She held her breath as the drone passed right by her. It continued on, deeper into the tunnel.

She waited a little longer, until the humming sound started to fade, before she slid out of hiding and ran down the tunnel towards the entrance, all the while cursing Jacob under her breath. *What was he thinking leaving the gate open!*

Kymara found Jacob eyeing off an old picture in a frame near the recycling dump. He turned to her. 'See. This is what I'm talking about. Classy.' His eye caught sight of an old rice cooker. 'Hey, look at this –'

Kymara stopped him. 'We don't have electricity, doofus. Leave it.'

He went to speak but she covered his mouth and gestured for him to follow her. She pointed to the sky. 'There are drones everywhere,' she said.

They started to make their way back to the tunnels. 'And there was one in the tunnel!' she said.

'Oh,' Jacob said. 'I left the gate open, didn't I?'

Kymara gave him a look that said everything.

'Sorry,' he said sheepishly, and the two started running as they heard the sound of humming once again getting closer.

•

From their vantage point behind the tree, Rose and Gemma were able to peer out and observe the action on the busy street on the bridge above as they kept a lookout for Mack. Suddenly they saw two Global Child Initiative officers approach the tree, and Gemma pulled Rose back, hiding from view.

Once the officers were out of hearing range, Rose turned to Gemma. 'Why are you so determined to rescue him? Knowing it's so dangerous?'

Gemma considered her response. 'There was something in his voice. He reminded me of how scared I was . . . so far from home. You all made me feel less alone.'

Rose stared at her for a moment. Then she smiled.

•

At home, Dru sat on the stairs as Kal stomped around in their bedroom. He'd read more of the Global Child Initiative manual and had decided to tidy his room, making sure his side was immaculate. Kal had even used red duct tape to make it clear that Dru wasn't welcome on his side of the room. Dru couldn't stand watching his brother behave this way. He tried the walkie-talkie. 'Come in, Unlisted. Are you there?'

There was no response. He tried the transceiver a second time.

'Unlisted, come in?'

•

'Can you hear me? Are you there? Over.'
Jacob and Kymara heard the crackle of the walkie-talkie down the tunnel and watched as a drone suddenly appeared. It moved closer to the abandoned walkie-talkie, which then fell silent, and the drone continued back on its trajectory along the tunnel.

Jacob and Kymara tentatively looked inside. Jacob

had the painting under his arm. 'How do we know it's safe?' he asked.

Kymara shrugged. 'No idea.'

Kymara glanced up and saw three teenage boys walking together a short distance away from the tunnel entrance. Kymara picked up an old apple core lying nearby and threw it at one of the boys before grabbing Jacob and hiding out of sight.

The boy turned around, eyes scouring the area for the source of the projectile. 'Which one of you jerks did that?' he asked his friends.

They laughed, and the sound drew the drone out from the tunnel, and Jacob and Kymara watched as it directed its attention to the three teenagers. They were all pushing and shoving each other by now, but when they saw the drone coming close to them, they all stopped, clearly alarmed at the sight.

Jacob and Kymara used the distraction to sprint into the tunnel entrance and back down to their hide-out. As they arrived Kymara heard the crackle of the walkie-talkie. She grabbed it. 'Hello?'

Dru was on the other end. 'It's great to hear your voice,' he said.

'What's up?' she said quickly. 'Are you okay?'

'I'm okay. Well, Kal's acting weird, but it's you guys I'm worried about.'

Jacob took the transceiver. 'Why?' he asked.

Dru explained what had happened at school. 'And they're doing a massive search for all the Unlisted.'

Jacob and Kymara nodded. 'Makes sense of the drones, then,' said Kymara dryly.

They heard a doorbell sound in the distance at Dru's end.

'I have to go,' Dru said. 'But you have to stay together. And don't leave the tunnels,' he warned before signing off.

Kymara and Jacob looked at one another. 'A bit late for that, I guess,' said Jacob with a shrug. He saw Kymara's concerned face. 'Help me find a place for my new artwork,' he said as he picked up the painting and tried it against the wall. 'What do you think?'

The distraction worked. Kymara cracked a smile.

CHAPTER NINETEEN

Kal came out of the bedroom and saw Dru carrying the walkie-talkie. 'If you spend all your time worrying about the Unlisted, you're going to lose your position as an Elite.'

Dru could hardly believe what he was hearing, 'I'm not Elite! I'm Unlisted too, remember?!'

The doorbell rang again, and they heard Dadi mumble something about having to answer it. Then Dadi's voice floated up from downstairs. 'Chloe! My girl! What's wrong?'

Kal immediately looked annoyed. He yelled down

the stairs. 'Dadi! Tell Chloe to go away! She's not allowed here.'

Dru glared at his twin brother in disbelief.

Kal tried to reason with his brother. 'Dru, she betrayed us. And she's a *Basic*.'

'What are you yapping on about?' Dadi said as she made her way up the stairs.

Kal continued quickly, 'I know a lot of what the Global Child Initiative is doing is messed up. But I've been reading the manual. Some of what they say makes sense.'

Dru couldn't believe what he was hearing. 'You're out of control!'

Kal wasn't backing down. 'I'll be honest, I enjoyed today. I liked being better than Chloe and the other kids.'

Just then a deafening cry came from the bedroom doorway. The boys turned to see a fierce-looking Dadi, with a teary Chloe next to her. Dadi growled, 'Say that again, wombat. I dare you.'

The boys had never seen her look so mad.

'We're not allowed to mix with –' started Kal but Dadi interrupted.

'Do you really think you're better than other children?'

Dru tried to make things better. 'Of course he doesn't.'

Dadi glared at her arrogant grandson. Everyone in the room knew that the lecture was far from over. She placed her hands firmly on her hips. 'This kind of segregation is the only thing I don't miss about India. Where some people are born being told they are worthless, while others are given the world!' She finished by yelling: 'In this house, everyone is equal!'

Kal had never been truly scared of Dadi until this very moment.

Dadi stopped to take a breath, then pointed at the red tape separating the two sides of the room. 'What's this?' she said, turning to Kal. 'You think you're too good for your brother now, too? Your *twin*? You have some difficult lessons to learn, Kalpen Sharma!'

She put her arm around Chloe and led her downstairs, offering freshly made samosas. Dru followed quickly after them.

Kal remained alone in the bedroom, unsure of what was happening to him. He'd thought he was right. He was convinced he had been. But now, with his grandmother so angry with him, he didn't know anymore.

•

Rose couldn't contain her yawn.

'Gemms, it's been over two hours,' she moaned. 'We need to head back.'

Gemma looked up at the bridge just as a large light blue motorhome pulled up, and an elderly couple stepped out and strolled up the street. Gemma was about to turn back to agree with Rose when she saw the back door open and a nervous-looking boy jump out, quite tall with curly red hair.

'I think that's him!' Gemma shrieked.

Rose moved to leave their hiding spot, but Gemma

grabbed her sleeve. 'What if I'm wrong?' she asked.

'I guess we'll find out,' said Rose as she pulled Gemma with her. As they approached the bridge, Gemma suddenly froze.

Rose looked at her friend. 'I'll go. Keep an eye on the road. And if you see anything, yell out and run.'

Gemma nodded, looking pale.

'I'll grab Mack and we'll head straight back to the tunnels, okay?'

'Okay,' whispered Gemma.

Rose ran up the stairs to the bridge and waved to catch Mack's attention.

Gemma watched from below, pleased to see them talking. She moved closer, finally breathing after holding her breath for so long, when a black van screeched to a stop behind Rose and Mack.

Gemma wanted to scream, tried to scream, but no noise came from her throat. She watched, petrified as two guards grabbed the teenagers, shoved them into the back of the van and drove off.

CHAPTER TWENTY

Rose's eyes opened, then closed again. She heard voices, but maybe they were just in her head. She opened her eyes again and a blinding white light flooded her vision. She was lying on a bed. She slowly sat up and looked around her as shapes came into focus and the brightness receded. She was wearing a jumpsuit and lying in a white room. She turned to her left and saw another bed. Mack was lying on it, wearing a matching white jumpsuit.

'Hey,' she said quietly. He didn't respond. She tried again. 'Hey!'

Mack stirred. He opened his eyes, looked at Rose. 'Where are we?'

'I don't know,' said Rose.

Mack slowly sat up and watched as Rose climbed off the bed and tried the door to the room, which was locked.

All of a sudden a voice boomed into the room via a speaker. 'Good morning, Rose and Mack. We are so glad that you could join us today.'

On the table near the door was a bottle of milk with two glasses. Mack and Rose walked to the table and sat down. And waited.

Soon the doors swung open and a woman strode into the room. She had dark hair pulled back into a bun, and shiny white teeth. She spoke in a soft, low, powerful voice. 'Rose. Mack. It's great to meet you in person – my name is Emma Ainsworth.' She extended her hand to shake hands with Mack.

Mack stared at it; his arms remained crossed.

The smile didn't slip from Emma's face. 'No? Fine. I'm the Chair of the Board here at the Global Child Initiative.'

'What do you want from us?' asked Rose, not bothering to keep the anger out of her voice.

'I'm here to help,' answered Emma in a sickly sweet voice. 'You were both missing for some time.'

'We're not afraid of you,' said Mack, sounding afraid. 'The others will come for us.'

Emma looked him straight in the eye. 'Others?' she said with interest.

'No. It's just the two of us,' corrected Rose.

But it was obvious the woman didn't believe her. Emma pulled out a tablet, and started showing photographs of missing kids. 'We're all on the same team here. Tell me, do you recognise any of these faces?'

The kids stayed silent.

'No? That's interesting. How about these faces?' She stood up and headed to the mirror on the wall. The mirror dissolved and became a window, revealing an adjacent waiting room where Rose's parents were seated. They were looking upset. Rose's mother's hands were clasped across her pregnant belly.

Rose let out a yelp and ran up to the glass. 'Mum? Dad!'

They showed no movement, and clearly could neither hear nor see her. Rose was frantic and Emma moved next to her, stroking her hair. 'You must miss them very much, Rose.'

A distraught Rose turned to Emma. 'Why are you doing this?'

'We want to find every missing child, and we need your help to do that. Once you've done that, you'll be free to go home with your parents.'

Rose looked longingly at her parents.

'But until you do, you'll need to stay here,' said Emma.

The window into the room turned back into a mirror, and Rose turned to face Emma. 'No! You can't do this!'

Emma smiled. 'I'll leave you to think it over.' She gestured to a blank sheet of paper and a pencil sitting on the table before she walked out of the room.

•

Kal had disappeared before Dru woke. The red tape had been removed – by Kal – before they'd gone to bed last night. But as Dru sat on the floor leaning against his bed, putting his shoes on, he knew that Kal still wasn't back to his normal self. It was finally the weekend though, which meant no creepy school rules to follow.

The walkie-talkie crackled, and he answered immediately. 'Hello?'

Kymara's panicked voice came over the airwaves. 'Rose and Gemma didn't come back last night! We're leaving the tunnels.'

'What?' said Dru.

Jacob's voice came through the transceiver. 'They were meeting another unlisted. We gotta go find them.'

'No!' hissed Dru. 'It's too dangerous. Stay where you are. What if they come back and you're not there? I'll come to you.'

Dru shoved the walkie-talkie and his laptop into his backpack and crept down the stairs. He had almost reached the front door when Kal came out from the kitchen, eating toast.

'I've got to go and see the Unlisted,' Dru whispered. 'Will you cover for me?'

Kal shrugged but didn't say no, so Dru opened the door – just as their aunt was about to knock.

'Ah, boys, there's something I need to show you,' she said as she opened a photo on her phone. 'I noticed they'd increased security in Room Four B . . . and I managed to get a photo when the guards were changing shifts.'

She showed the boys the screen: Rose and a boy, both dressed in white jumpsuits sitting in a white room.

'They got Rose!' Dru cried.

Kal looked at the screen, emotionless. 'I guess it's out of our hands now.'

Maya looked at him in astonishment.

'I have to go,' Dru said as he headed out the front door. 'Bua, can you send me that photo?' He took the walkie-talkie from his backpack and handed it to Kal. 'Keep this. I'll call from the tunnels if we need help.'

Kal took the walkie-talkie and wandered back to the kitchen. 'Whatever.'

•

Kymara and Jacob were taking turns pacing up and down their hide-out when, all of a sudden, a distressed and exhausted Gemma arrived back.

They were so relieved to see her they rushed over to give her a hug.

'Are you okay?' asked Kymara.

'Where have you been?' asked Jacob.

'And where's Rose and Mack?' added Kymara.

Gemma was barely able to speak. She began to sob, but caught her breath at the sound of heavy footsteps behind them. 'They're here. Get down!' she hissed. The three teens dropped to the floor.

'What are you all doing on the ground?' Dru said as he entered the hide-out. There were sighs of relief as they got up, dusting themselves off as Dru continued. 'They've got Rose. And the other kid. I'm glad you weren't caught too, Gemma.'

Kymara and Jacob turned to Gemma for answers. Tears streamed down her face as she told them what happened, about the black van.

A heavy silence filled the room after she finished. Gemma was obviously racked with guilt. 'I'm the reason Rose was out there in the first place. I froze. This is all my fault.'

Kymara stared at Gemma. 'Yeah, it is,' she said angrily.

Jacob whacked Kymara's arm. 'Ow!' said Kymara, glaring at him.

Dru grabbed his laptop. 'They're being held at Global Child Initiative headquarters, where my Aunt Maya works,' he said. He opened the laptop and showed them the photo Maya had sent through. There they were: Rose and Mack in the white room.

'I can't handle this,' Gemma said. 'I have to do something!' Half-crazed, she turned and ran out of the chamber.

'Gemma, stop! Where are you going?' cried out Jacob.

But Gemma was gone.

Jacob and Kymara started to follow her, but Dru stopped them. 'You shouldn't leave the tunnels. It's not safe. I'll go.' He gestured to the walkie-talkie in Kymara's hand. 'I'll need Kal. Can I take that?'

Kymara handed it over and Dru dashed out of the tunnels after Gemma.

CHAPTER TWENTY-ONE

Kal lay on his back in the backyard. He tossed a basketball as high as he could and watched it travel swiftly back towards him, catching it at the last moment.

'Excuse me, little wombat,' Dadi said, appearing with a basket of washing. 'I don't want to interrupt your very important business,' she said sarcastically.

'That's okay,' said Kal.

'If it's not too much trouble could you help your dadi by hanging out this washing that should have gone on the line two hours ago?'

Before he could answer she dumped the laundry

basket on him. 'Much appreciated,' she said as she walked back towards the house.

Kal groaned. What teenager liked hanging out washing? It was something Dru normally did. But with Dru chasing after the Unlisted . . . Kal sat up, annoyed by his brother's selfishness.

A door slammed across the road and Kal watched as Chloe trudged down her front path carrying a hefty garbage bag. She dumped the bag in the bin and then saw Kal staring at her. She glared at him, and then stormed off up her driveway.

Kal reached into the laundry basket to start hanging out the clothes when the screech of bike tyres distracted him. He looked up to see Regan standing with her bike on the footpath in front of the Sharma's house. '*Laundry?* What are you doing? We're gonna be late.'

'Late for what?' he asked blankly.

'The Adrenoblast Action Zone is launching in an hour.'

Kal shrugged. 'I'll wait until there's no queue.'

Regan laughed at him. 'Elites don't queue,' she said as though it were obvious.

'Oh, I should probably wait for Dru.'

Regan rolled her eyes, teasing. 'You can't do anything without Dru.' She climbed back on her bike. 'You decide, Sharma. Washing or Adrenoblast.'

She rode off.

Kal made a quick decision. He stashed the laundry basket behind a tree and ran back into the house to grab his bag. There were awesome games to be played!

•

Regan was right. They didn't have to queue. They were treated like VIPs as they walked into the Adrenoblast zone, bypassing the long queue of disgruntled kids. Once inside, Kal was taken in by all the games he could play for free. There was laser tag, escape rooms, video games he didn't realise had even been released yet. He walked past people playing e-sports, testing out new gadgets, watching electronic displays.

There were so many activities to choose from he

couldn't pick what he wanted to play first. He walked towards a VR gaming booth, dumped his backpack and put on the gaming glasses. In the side pocket of his backpack, the walkie-talkie crackled.

•

Gemma had taken a lot of back roads to avoid being seen, but eventually she arrived at Global Child Initiative headquarters. She noticed a fire exit she thought she might be able to get in through, and was heading towards it when she felt a hand on her shoulder.

She turned, terrified, to see Dru behind her. 'You followed me?' she said, not bothering to hide her annoyance.

'You're going to get yourself caught!' Dru snapped back, equally annoyed by her erratic behaviour. 'We can't stay here out in the open,' he added. 'There's my aunt's car. We'll see if she left it unlocked.'

It seemed unlikely, but Gemma didn't have a better idea to offer, so the two teenagers ran towards the car. It was locked. Gemma shook the car handle in frustration, and the alarm went off.

'What are you doing now?!' shouted Dru over the blare. 'We have to get out of here before security arrives!'

'I'm not going anywhere without Rose!' yelled back Gemma.

But then they spotted Maya leaving the building, aiming her car key to turn off the alarm, but it wasn't working. She reached the driver's side and turned the alarm off, taking a quick look around the car, trying to figure out why the alarm had sounded in the first place. She walked around the other side of the car and stopped when she saw her nephew and Gemma crouching, looking guilty.

She looked around quickly. 'This place is crawling with security guards,' she said to them, furious. 'What were you thinking?'

'We need your help to get inside,' said Gemma.

Maya scoffed. 'So they can lock you up too? No way.'

'I knew I couldn't trust an adult. I'll do it myself.'

Gemma went to make a run for it but Maya stopped her. Dru pleaded with his aunt. 'Please, Bua. You have to help us. Promise you'll do something to help them.'

Maya glanced up to see a uniformed guard crossing the carpark. 'All right. I promise. Now get out of here.'

At that moment the guard called out. 'Everything all right, Dr Sharma?'

Maya straightened her back as she turned to him, her composure regained. 'Sorry. False alarm.' She smiled warmly at the officer as he escorted her back towards the side door of the building.

Dru and Gemma waited a few moments longer and then ran out of the carpark.

•

Back at Adrenoblast, Regan and Kal were having a blast. After playing air hockey and competing in a rally-car driving game, they decided they had earnt lunch. They sat at a table near a window that looked out onto Darling Harbour, and they watched the water sparkle in the sunlight as sushi was brought to their table. They tucked in, famished. It was a terrific view and a delicious lunch after an awesome day of gaming. If this was Elite-style living, Kal wanted in. 'I'm wiped,' he said with a big smile. 'This place is amazing. I can't believe all the cool stuff we get.'

Regan beamed. 'You better start believing, Kal.'

Suddenly, the walkie-talkie crackled loudly from Kal's backpack. He didn't want this amazing feeling ruined by his needy brother. He glared at the walkie-talkie but said nothing.

Regan looked at Kal, an eyebrow raised. 'Is that Dru? What does he want?'

Kal rolled his eyes, 'Don't worry about him, he's such a nerd. Still loves playing with walkie-talkies.' He reached over to the walkie-talkie and turned it off. Or he thought he had, but he bumped it back on when he returned it to the side pocket of his bag, which meant that Dru could hear everything that was said from that moment on.

Regan leaned in closer to Kal. 'Can I give you a word of warning about Dru?' she said conspiratorially.

Kal didn't reply. She continued, 'I know he's your brother or whatever, but he's not Elite material. Sooner or later they're gonna move him down to Core – or even Basic – and when they do, you'll have to make a choice. If you want to keep all of this.' She gestured to the food and the games and the promise of an Elite future.

Kal's eyes widened as an attendant placed a huge piece of black forest gateau in front of him and Regan and emptied away the old plates.

Kal looked down at the cake. 'Hey,' he said, 'if Dru's stupid enough to lose all this, then I'm not going down with him.'

Regan nodded happily and the two of them began eating the cake.

•

'I'm sure he didn't mean that,' said Jacob as he watched Dru's reaction to his brother's heartless comments.

Gemma, though, didn't bother to try to make Dru feel better. 'If Kal can turn on you like that, what's he gonna do to us?' she challenged.

Dru tried to explain, even though he felt completely gutted. 'It's not Kal, it's the implant. It's shutting down all his feelings. And whatever they're doing to him, it's getting worse.'

He handed back the walkie-talkie to the Unlisted. 'I better be getting home. I'll be in touch, okay?'

The others waved goodbye and headed back into the tunnels as Dru jumped on his bike and began the ride home. Dru wished for a moment his feelings could be shut down too. It was becoming harder and harder to deal with the constant fear and worry about the twin who was becoming a stranger to him.

CHAPTER TWENTY-TWO

The blank piece of paper and pencil sat untouched on the table in the white room. Rose couldn't bring herself to write anything on it. She desperately wanted to be with her parents, but there wasn't a chance she could tell Emma Ainsworth where her friends were hiding out. It was an impossible situation.

Rose looked at the mirrored wall, wondering if her parents were still sitting on the other side.

Mack could see she was hurting. 'Maybe if you write something they'll let you see your parents.'

Rose slowly picked up the pencil. She looked up at

Mack and a wave of suspicion hit her. 'Why do you want me to write something?'

Mack looked surprised. 'What? I don't. I just thought –'

'Are you one of them?' Rose asked harshly.

'No!' Mack cried.

Rose hardly knew this boy but she could see he was scared.

'I've been in hiding this whole time, like you.'

Rose jumped to her to feet. 'How did the Global Child Initiative know about our meeting?'

Mack was looking pale now, and his hands started to shake. 'I don't know! I'm telling you the truth!'

Suddenly, Rose picked up the pencil and threw it at him. 'Hey, catch this!' He reached for the pencil half a second too late, and it bounced off him, falling to the floor.

It was obvious he had no enhanced powers, and the look on his face made it clear he was hurt by her behaviour.

'I'm sorry, Mack. This place is messing with my head.'

The door of the white room opened and Emma and a security guard entered. 'Unfortunately we have run out of time,' said Emma, sounding disappointed.

The security guard stepped up to Rose and held out his hand. 'Your locket.'

Rose shakily removed the necklace from around her neck and gave it to the guard. He dropped it on the floor and stepped hard on it, breaking it into pieces. He then picked it up and put the broken pieces in a plastic evidence bag and handed it to Emma. She smiled and walked calmly out of the room. The guard followed, and the door locked behind them.

Suddenly the mirror dissolved and Rose watched helplessly through the glass as Emma held out the broken locket to her parents. Rose's mother collapsed in tears, held up by her distraught father.

Rose yelled at the glass, banging her hands against it. 'Mum! Dad! I'm here! I'm right here!' Tears streamed down her face.

But her parents couldn't hear her, nor could they

see her. Slowly the glass turned back into a mirror, leaving Rose staring at her own tear-stained face.

•

In another part of the Global Child Initiative headquarters Maya Sharma walked down a hallway, carrying a clipboard. She was about to pass a security guard when she stumbled, dropping her clipboard and sending papers flying across the floor.

'Oh, that's just great,' she said as she smiled apologetically at the guard. He crouched to help her gather the papers and while he was doing so, Maya reached over and snatched the security card from his belt as he leant forward. He handed her the papers, unaware he'd just been robbed. She stood up, nodded to the guard and walked quickly away.

•

Rose was slumped on the white floor, sitting against the white wall, crying. Mack was trying his best to comfort her, but nothing he said seemed to make her feel better. Just as he was about to speak again, her sobs became louder, and he kept quiet. Instead he simply sat down next to her. Neither of them could know what was in store, and there was nothing else to do. So, they sat there, hopeless and helpless. Mack closed his eyes, and soon Rose's eyelids fluttered shut too, but they pinged open suddenly when she heard the sound of something being slid under the door.

Mack startled too, and they both looked to the door: on the floor was what looked like a security card. They looked at each other, amazed.

'Is it a trap?' asked Mack, looking up at the surveillance camera in the corner of the room.

'Who cares if it is?' said Rose, coming to life once more. She wiped away her tears and grabbed the card. She turned to Mack. 'Let's get out of here!'

There was a panel on the side of the door, and Rose swiped the pass card. The door automatically opened. But instead of burly looking security guards ready to descend, the corridor was empty. Rose and Mack looked cautiously up and down. Rose, with hopeful anticipation, immediately ran into the room next door where she had seen her parents – but it was empty.

Rose felt a fresh wave of devastation. Her parents were gone. They'd been so close, and it felt like weeks since she'd last been hugged by them. The thought was enough to make her sink back down to the floor and cry some more. But Mack grabbed her by the hand. 'We should keep moving,' he said.

Rose took a steadying breath and nodded. Giving up would not do them any good.

Because both she and Mack had entered the facility unconscious, they had no memory of where to go. So they just had to take their chances. Down a corridor they ran, and then the next one, and the next one. The place was eerily empty. There were no windows, so they didn't even know if it was day or night.

They reached a larger corridor in what seemed less like a hospital and more like a corporate office area, and Rose tried a door. It didn't open.

They heard voices coming from further up the

corridor. Rose quickly moved along to the second door and desperately tried the door handle. It opened! They both scrambled inside and shut the door behind them, too scared to move.

They heard footsteps move past; they didn't stop. Mack stood guard by the door as Rose approached a large desk in the centre of the room. A USB stuck out of one of several computers, and Rose grabbed it. One half was made of a shiny crystal material on the side of which was printed a holographic Infinity Group logo. She was about to ask Mack whether they should try to find out what was on the USB when he gestured desperately from his place near the door.

Rose joined him and they leaned against the door. They heard voices coming closer, one female and one male. Rose quickly pocketed the USB and hid with Mack against the wall, just as the office door swung open. The door hid them from sight, which was lucky, because the light switch was turned on, and fluorescent tube lighting flooded the room.

As the two adjusted to the bright lights, they saw

Emma Ainsworth and a man in a suit walk towards the desk. She opened up a presentation on a screen on the back wall and he took a seat.

Emma remained standing and started her speech. 'Over the past few weeks we have rolled out rigorous testing across the nation.'

The man nodded enthusiastically. 'It's good to see things are back on track after the situation in China.'

Rose saw Emma flinch at the man's mention of China, but her calm voice didn't waver. 'A momentary glitch. The first batch of prototypes will be officially unveiled to you and your fellow investors next week at The Global Child Congress.'

'Excellent news,' said the investor.

'As you know,' Emma continued, 'this will be the final stage of our experiment, when we move to complete permanent mind control. Within five years, the next generation of fully compliant employees will be entering the workforce. You won't be disappointed.' She beamed with pride.

While the two adults were concentrating on the

presentation, Rose and Mack crawled from behind the door and moved to the entrance. Just as they were about to make their escape, Mack bumped into the door and it hit the wall.

Emma and the investor looked over to see Mack and Rose clambering to stand.

'Run!' Rose cried and the two raced off down the corridor.

Within seconds Emma Ainsworth's voice was heard echoing through the building over the loudspeaker. 'Attention all security personnel.'

Meanwhile, Mack and Rose sprinted down corridors until they came to an exit door. Pushing on it, they stumbled outside into the sunshine, and ran towards the carpark.

'Which way should we go, Rose?' asked Mack, sounding panicked.

Rose looked around, trying to get her bearings. 'I don't know.' She stopped for a moment, thinking.

Mack pleaded with her. 'Rose? We have to keep moving!'

Rose shook her head, puzzled. 'You saw the security in that place. Why aren't there guards here?'

Mack looked around. It did feel odd. Then they heard a loud, low buzzing sound. A single drone appeared. And then another, and another. They hovered near Rose and Mack, poised and waiting.

Rose took a deep breath, made a decision, and sat down right where she was, resigned and defiant.

Mack stood still, frozen.

The drones kept watch as the teenagers stayed put. It didn't take long for a car with tinted windows to pull up alongside them. The passenger door opened to reveal Emma in her crisp white suit. 'Well, that's disappointing. I was hoping you would lead me to your friends. Still, an incredibly bold escape . . . I think you'll both do very well in our athletics program.'

Emma clapped her hands and two guards, who were waiting nearby, stepped up and took hold of the two escapees.

CHAPTER TWENTY-THREE

At the Sharma house the family was finishing up dinner. But Kal had been talking so much about how amazing Adrenoblast had been, he had hardly started eating. Dru was glowering at him but Kal didn't seem to notice. 'It was *so* cool. They had indoor ultimate frisbee and these hyper-realistic VR games!' he enthused. 'And then we went through to this amazing restaurant where all the food was free.'

Finally Dru had had enough of his brother's insensitivity. He stood up and started clearing the table, beginning with Kal's largely uneaten meal.

'All finished?' He snatched Kal's plate and marched towards the sink.

Kal was caught off-guard. 'Hey! I was still eating that!'

Dru ignored his twin and unceremoniously dumped the rest of Kal's food in the bin. Although the boys' mum and dad noticed the tension between the two, Rahul was still pleased that Dru was clearing the table. 'Brilliant, looks like Dru's on wash-up duty. Who wants to catch the second half of *Cake Bake*?'

He didn't have to ask twice; the rest of the family immediately followed Rahul out to the TV room. But Kal stayed behind and confronted his brother. 'Why did you take away my food before I'd finished it?'

Dru turned to Kal, eyes flashing in anger. 'Why don't you ask your good mate Regan to save you some dinner? Something better suited to *Elites*?'

Kal looked momentarily confused.

'I heard everything you said to her. About how I'm some loser you'll throw away to keep your stupid Elite status,' he said.

Kal held up his hands in a defensive stance. 'You don't understand, Dru –'

Dru gritted his teeth. 'No, I *do* understand. You're totally one of them now! And the worst part is – you're enjoying it.'

Kal attempted to reason with his brother. 'Look, Dru. I didn't ask for this. I especially didn't ask for it twice. You can't be angry at me for enjoying one day when I spend every other day worrying that they're going to take control of my brain.'

Despite Dru's anger, he couldn't help but admit that Kal had made a fair point. But that didn't excuse him from ignoring Dru when he'd needed his help. Dru plunged his hands into the soapy water and scrubbed plates as he thought some more. Actually, he'd managed fine without his brother. And he was aware that Kal hated not being in control of what was going on in his head. He looked up at his brother, less angry.

Kal smiled. 'Anyway, you know what they say: keep your friends close and your enemies closer.' The brothers called a truce, and shook on it. But one of the boys knocked a glass off the bench and it smashed on the floor.

From the other room Dadi called out. 'Careful, wombats!' Kal grinned mischievously and hollered back. 'It was Dru!'

'Well, make sure you take that dust pan and clean everything up. We don't want broken glass in your feet now,' continued Dadi, still shouting from the other room.

'Sh!' said Vidya. 'We're trying to watch TV, Dadi.'

'Don't shush your dadi,' said Anousha.

'Sh,' said Rahul. 'Everyone be quiet.'

Dru went to flick a tea towel at Kal but he sprinted out of the kitchen, laughing. 'I don't want to miss *Cake Bake*,' Kal called out to his brother as though it were the most important thing in his life.

Dru laughed, for what felt like the first time in weeks. For a moment it was just a normal night at home with his family. It felt good. Even though he'd been left with all the washing up and a broken glass to pick up.

•

At the Global Child Initiative headquarters Maya Sharma was working late, as she had done most nights since she had taken on this new job. She stifled a yawn and looked at her watch. She usually tried to get over to her brother's house so the whole Sharma family could enjoy *Cake Bake* together. It was a silly show, but Rahul, being a baker, loved every moment of it, and the running commentary from all the family made it a hilarious hour of quality family time.

She looked at the cold, sterile environment that was now her work home. The buzz of a fluorescent light overhead seemed to be getting louder and louder. She didn't want to be here anymore, but Dru and Kal had convinced her she needed to stay in her position so as not to arouse suspicion. But she wasn't sure what she could do to stop what was happening, and she certainly didn't want to be responsible for hurting any children. She thought back to Jiao; had he survived the flight back to China? Was he okay?

Maya's thoughts then drifted to Rose and the

red-headed boy who had been locked in the white room earlier in the day, and the card she had slipped under the door. Perhaps she had managed to help them. At the very least she had given them a chance to slip away, but she couldn't know if they had succeeded.

She'd purposefully stayed out of everyone's way, and spent most of the afternoon unpacking medical equipment and stacking shelves in the laboratory. Some of the equipment she'd unboxed wasn't standard and she didn't want to think too closely about what some of the larger needles she'd found in the storeroom might be used for.

She finished unpacking the last box and yawned. It was time to go home.

But suddenly Emma Ainsworth appeared out of nowhere, surprising Maya with an intense stare.

Maya smiled nervously. 'Oh, Ms Ainsworth! I'm sorry about my yawning. It's been a long day. I didn't expect to see you here this late.'

Emma delivered a frosty look and didn't bother with niceties. She was like a shark circling her prey.

'Dr Sharma. There was a security breach on Level One today. The system shows that you were in that area. Did you see anything suspicious?'

Maya swallowed hard. 'No, I – I don't think so. I didn't see anything.'

Emma paused and held eye contact with Maya, who smiled awkwardly and folded up the flaps of the empty box, ready to take it away.

But Emma stepped closer to Maya and lowered her voice. 'We value our employees' loyalty here at the Initiative, Dr Sharma. And sometimes it's worth seeing loyalty in action. Would you mind coming with me?'

Maya carefully put down the box and responded, 'Uh . . . not at all.'

Emma motioned for Maya to follow. Maya had no idea what she was in for, but she was pretty sure it wasn't going to be a friendly coffee and a chat about the weather. Time seemed to slow down as the two women walked down a corridor towards a white curtain.

Emma pulled back the curtain to reveal Rose tied

to a dentist's chair. Dr Wender was preparing a large dentist's drill with an implant. A short distance away, Mack was also tied down, looking terrified. He was obviously going to be implanted after Rose.

'This won't hurt for long,' said Dr Wenders.

Emma gently tapped Dr Wenders on the arm. 'Doctor Sharma will handle this one.'

Dr Wenders paused, then nodded to Emma. He handed the large drill to Maya, who reluctantly took it. Now that she knew what the implant was doing to these children, it took all her professional ability not to throw the drill on the floor and run. But she knew that wouldn't help Rose, or the boy, or herself. So, sweat beading on her forehead, she reached down, closer to Rose's terrified face.

Emma said impatiently, 'We don't have all night, Dr Sharma.'

Maya held the drill over Rose's face. 'Open your mouth.'

Rose pleaded with her eyes not to let this happen, but Maya felt helpless.

'You heard what the doctor said, Rose. Now, be a good girl and open your mouth.'

Rose opened her mouth, her eyes wide with terror as Maya placed the drill near her gum.

'I'm so sorry, Rose,' Maya whispered before switching on the drill.

IT'S NOT OVER FOR THE UNLISTED.

Read on for a sneak peek of Book Three: *Sabotage*.

CHAPTER ONE

It was mid-morning in the Sharma house. Identical Indian–Australian twins Kal and Dru entered the kitchen, coming face to face with an old man, who looked a bit like their father. He was seated at the kitchen table, which was covered with brushes, powders and other make-up. Their older sister Vidya was picking up a make-up brush from a pouch when she turned and saw her brothers' faces.

Using his best grandpa voice, Rahul asked, 'How do you like your old man?'

Their confused expressions made their sister and father laugh.

Dru looked to Vidya. 'You did this?'

'Why are you so surprised?' asked Vidya. 'I've been studying stage make-up all year. And Dad's being my model for my character assignment which is due tomorrow.'

Kal peered up close at Rahul. 'It's good how you've managed to make Dad look really ancient,' he said, impressed.

'Really ancient but also really handsome, no?' said Rahul with a gleam in his eye.

Dadi bustled around the kitchen, filling a tiffin with prepared food. 'Why waste your talent making my son look so old? Why not make your dadi look young?'

Vidya knew exactly what to say in a situation like this. 'But Dadi – people already think you're my sister!'

Dadi smiled at her granddaughter but then, just as quickly, frowned. 'Can you believe they're making my poor daughter work all weekend? Dru, I'll need your help to take your bua's lunch to her.'

The twins' aunt, a doctor, had recently started working for the Global Child Initiative (GCI), which she had thought was a wonderful organisation created to help children receive the best health care available, all around the world. But the shady parent company Infinity Group was behind the Initiative, and rather than altruistic aims, something much more sinister had come into play. The GCI rolled out 'dental checks' to schools all over Australia – it wasn't a normal dental check though. Infinity Group had used the appointments to implant every child with a device that could be tracked, giving the company the ability to know where every implanted child was at any given time, and – even more frighteningly – to influence their thoughts and actions.

Dru and Kal were some of the only people aware of what was really going on, all because of Dru's terror of the dentist. He had convinced his brother to pretend to be him for the check-up, not realising that this meant Kal had been implanted twice.

When the students at Westbrook High started

to behave strangely – group loss of consciousness, increased strength and enhanced language skills – Dru and Kal had started to investigate what was really going on.

Because Dru hadn't been implanted, he was not being brainwashed like his brother and all the other kids in their class. Through their investigative work the twins had discovered other 'Unlisted' kids who had not gone to the dental check-up or received the implant. The twins had befriended four runaways – Kymara, Rose, Jacob and Gemma – who had been hiding out in the tunnels of St James train station, and had helped them as much as they could. But Rose had been captured and was now imprisoned at GCI headquarters, which was where the twins' dadi was suggesting they go for a nice Sunday outing to see their aunt.

'Oh, you hear that, Kal?' Dru said. 'A trip to Global Child Initiative headquarters.'

Kal shrugged, non-committal.

'Maybe we should both go,' suggested Dru with

a meaningful look at his twin. Dru needed Kal near him at headquarters because otherwise they might find out he wasn't being tracked.

'Sure,' said Kal, unenthused.

'Both my wombats! What a treat,' said Dadi. 'Kal, please fetch the umbrellas.'

Kal looked out the window. The sun was shining. 'But there's not a cloud in the sky.'

'Believe your dadi,' she said in her wise-woman voice. 'A storm is coming.'

Dru swallowed hard at his grandmother's ominous words.

Dadi drove the two boys into the city, and they were soon at the front entrance of Global Child Initiative headquarters. The twins had been there a few days earlier with their school group, taking part in an organised scavenger hunt – but the results weren't exactly what the GCI official planned, with another Unlisted boy, a Chinese exchange student named Jiao, being captured and taken away. These were not good memories, and the boys weren't happy to be back again so soon.

Dadi looked up, oblivious to the boys' discomfort. 'My, my, look at this impressive building, boys,' she said. 'If you work hard at school, you might be able to get a job in a place like this too.'

The boys shared a horrified look. This was literally the last place they would want to work. Ever.

Dadi, wearing a bright sari, bustled through the entrance towards the metal detector until she was stopped by a security guard. The tiffins were metal and had to be checked separately.

'What's this?' asked the security guard suspiciously.

Dadi pulled out the tiffin. 'Lunch for my daughter, of course,' she said indignantly. 'She's working. On a Sunday.'

'She's not the only one,' said the guard unsympathetically.

Kal and Dru passed through the metal detector together.

'Open the lunch, please,' instructed the guard.

The boys noticed a second security guard holding a handheld implant scanner, stationed near the stairs.

Dadi opened the first compartment of the tiffin. A delicious aroma rose from the still-warm samosas.

The security guard sighed. 'That smells sensational. I'm supposed to be on a diet, but –'

'Take one,' Dadi said graciously. 'I have plenty.'

The guard did not need to be asked twice. He grabbed a samosa and bit into it, moaning in appreciation as Dadi opened a small container of raita. 'And this is my special mint chutney.'

The guard dipped his samosa in the chutney before popping it in his mouth. 'Oh, even better.'

He waved Dadi through the scanner, and she and the twins approached the reception desk, passing a small group of adults seated in the foyer.

Dadi said to the receptionist, 'Could you please tell Dr Sharma her mother and nephews are here with her lunch?'

The receptionist nodded and called Maya Sharma's extension. While they were waiting, a middle-aged woman with a blonde bob, wearing a white shirt and black trousers approached the reception desk. 'Hello. I'm here for the Super Recogniser training day.'

The receptionist gestured to the other seated adults. 'Wait over there with the others,' she instructed.

Dru's attention was caught by a screen that displayed images of missing children along with the text: *Have you seen these children? Every child deserves a better future.*

Dru looked at Kal and nodded to the board. Kal shrugged. 'We're here to find out about Rose. Don't lose focus.'

Maya appeared in the foyer, looking weary and drawn.

'Oh my girl,' said Dadi sympathetically. 'You look so tired. Luckily, I've brought you a nutritious lunch.'

'Thank you, Mum,' said Maya, giving her a hug. 'Hello boys.' She gave them a lingering, pointed look, and Kal immediately took the hint.

'Dadi,' he said, 'I think that guard looks like he'd really like another samosa. You should give him one.'

'Good idea, my wombat,' said Dadi with a grin. She

picked up one with a serviette and walked with Kal over to the guard, who greeted Dadi like a long-lost relative when he saw what she was bringing him.

Maya quietly relayed the information she knew Dru would be desperate to hear. 'Your friends tried to escape last night. But Emma Ainsworth brought them back in.'

'What? Where are they keeping them?' asked Dru.

'Level one,' answered Maya before frowning. 'Don't even think about it, Dru. I'll figure something out. But there's something else I need to . . .' She lost her train of thought as she noticed the Super Recognisers. Concern flashed across her face.

Dru followed her gaze. 'What's the matter, Bua? Who are they?'

'They're called Super Recognisers. They're people who've been tested and found to have a natural ability to recall any face in an instant. The Initiative plans to hire hundreds of them.'

'Why?' asked Dru.

'They're determined to find every child who missed

the dental check – these Super Recognisers will help track them down.'

Dru was horrified, but there was no time to say anything else as Dadi returned with Kal. 'Let's go, boys. I can feel that storm getting closer.'

After saying goodbye to Maya, Dru, Kal and Dadi headed back outside in the direction of their car. They passed an electrical substation, with hazard and general construction signs erected outside.

'Why do you hate storms so much, Dadi?' asked Kal.

Dadi shook her head. 'No, no, Kal. I love storms. They are a message from Indra, the King of Heaven, promising to lend his power to protect those who cry out for his help. This is all good. What I don't love so much is getting wet,' she concluded wisely.

As the family passed the substation they saw a workman outside. Dadi looked at him, concerned. 'Sir, you should be careful. An almighty thunderstorm is coming.'

The workman looked at the sky just at the moment they all heard a distant rumble of thunder. 'Thanks for the heads-up. You don't want to be anywhere near here if that substation gets hit by lightning. It'll take out the whole grid.'

Dru looked at the substation, an idea forming. He turned to the workman. 'Could you show us what you're doing? My brother would be really interested. He wants to become an electrical engineer.'

Dadi turned to Kal in surprise. 'Is this true?'

Kal wasn't sure what Dru was up to but knew he had to play along. 'Um, yes . . .'

Dadi looked thoughtful. 'Well, then. You'll need to study much harder.'

The workman shook his head. 'Sorry, I can't really let the public in.'

Now that Dadi realised this was an educational opportunity for her grandson, she was not going to take no for an answer. 'Oh, come on, sir. A quick peek for a budding electrical engineer?' Dadi flashed her winning smile.

The workman relented and let them in. 'Okay. But just for a second.' He stepped into the cramped substation, which was full of cables, switches and transformers. The twins joined him while Dadi stayed outside, looking up at the sky with a frown.

Inside, the workman pointed to some cables. 'Over there are some pretty standard high-voltage transmission lines.'

Kal shot a bewildered look to Dru but played along, nodding enthusiastically as Dru slipped away and looked around.

'Wow, that's amazing,' said Kal.

The workman was so delighted by Kal's interest he continued to talk nonstop. 'It all operates with a three-phase alternating current through a synchronised grid.'

'So interesting,' said Kal, looking as though he'd rather hang washing on the line than listen to this guy talk about electricity a moment longer.

While the workman continued educating Kal, Dru took a casual walk around the substation. He scanned the mass of cables and wires.

'The power runs into the substation at a

transmission-level voltage, but then of course it's stepped down to distribution-level voltage so it can go out to the distribution wiring. Now, as I'm sure you will have ascertained, each service location on the grid has its own required service voltage.'

Dru grabbed a document labelled 'Grid Service Manual' and flicked quickly through it. There were instructions on the substation and a map of the facilities. Perfect! Dru hid the manual under his T-shirt and moved back out to join his brother near the entrance.

Another rumble of thunder sounded.

'Wow, that was all *so* interesting, but we have to go now,' said Dru as he quickly pulled his brother away.

Dadi smiled at the workman.

'Thank you so much. And don't for get the storm. It's on it's way.'